book one of the beasts trilogy

MOONSTEED

manda benson

www.tangentrine.com

www.tangentrine.com

Third edition published by Tangentrine 2024
Second edition published by Kensington 2014
First published by Lyrical Press 2011

British Library Cataloguing in Publication Data. A catalogue record for this book is available from the British Library.

This novel is a work of fiction. Any resemblance to locations, incidents, or persons living or dead is purely coincidental.

Moonsteed and its respective characters are the intellectual property of Manda Benson. All rights reserved. No part of this publication may be reproduced, stored in a retrieval system, or transmitted in any form or by any means, electronic, mechanical, photocopying, recording, or otherwise, without the prior permission of the publishers.

Copyright © Manda Benson 2010

Manda Benson asserts the moral right to be identified as the author of this work.

Cover image of Jupiter © ESA/Hubble, used under Creative Commons licence.

ISBN: 978-0-9566080-6-2

BEASTS

moonsteed

sunhawk

starhound

For Zarcan

and with thanks to

Nerine Dorman
and
DJ Cockburn

chapter one

I T'S EASY TO FALL off a horse in 0.126 g.

Verity dug knees hard into the saddle, shifting her balance into the motion as the horse veered and leapt to clear a crater.

On the other hand, at least hitting the ground doesn't hurt so much.

The horse touched down and recovered its stride, the lamps on the breastplate and Verity's helmet casting a quivering figure-eight on the black ice ahead. The fleeing horse and the man who had stolen it were some distance before them, lost in the oblique shadows of the towering ice protrusions cast by the light of a shrunken sun low on the horizon.

Verity thought-prompted the research base's ANT. The spy was still in range of the tracking systems, and their feedback indicated he continued on a course towards the scarp. "Private Aaron, are you still following me?" she said into the receiver of her helmet. Aaron's voice came back confirming, and she glanced over her shoulder to check his position. He was a recent recruit, she recalled, John Aaron, a dull, ordinary name, and it suited him. He rode poorly, hunched forward, his weight in his seat, not in the stirrups. Having him along with her could very well turn out worse than taking on this pursuit alone.

"If he tries to lose us up the scarp, we're in for a hard ride," Verity said. "Ideally we need him alive, but whatever happens we mustn't shoot him. The voltage will fry his nervous system and the Inquisitor won't be able to get anything out of his brain."

After a pause during which Verity thought she heard Aaron cursing under his breath into his transmitter, his reply came back, "Understood."

Clouds of vapour rushed from the horse's nostrils with

each exhalation, but Callisto's atmosphere froze it into crystals of ice that clung to Verity's knees and the armour protecting the horse's neck. Far ahead, the figure of the fugitive upon his horse came into view, racing to the edge of the scarp. The spy was taking the long route. Verity knew the scarp well, and this was not the only way.

"You, follow him," she ordered Aaron. "I'm going to see if I can cut him off. Don't rush and don't take any risks you don't have to."

Verity turned the horse towards the base of the scarp. This area of Callisto was geologically newer than the dark plain that lay behind her. An impact from space that must have occurred around the time of the terraforming had blown a crater in the surface and forced an eruption of liquid water from the crust surrounding it, creating a ridge covered in jagged ice formations. A pale mountain reached into the sky ahead, facets of jutting ice glittering from the heights in Jupiter's russet-tinged light. She braced herself again as the horse gathered itself to jump a fissure. The lamps illuminated more cracks in the stratum, some of them wide and sprouting ice spears. The horse cleared them easily. Verity made out details on the steep slope ahead, and began planning the course they'd take up it.

At her thought-prompt to the horse's cybernetic armour, razor-sharp crampons extruded from the shoes to grip the stratum. Verity seated herself firmly, gripping with her knees, and gave the thought-prompt to the horse to jump.

The first leap carried them twenty feet up to a ledge above some pointed stalagmites. A few beats of a canter, then the next jump, and the next, and so Verity guided the horse towards the summit. The horse moved as one with her, and she felt the ice under her feet and saw the world through its eyes, a wide, panoramic vision strangely devoid of red hues. The horse could feel no fear, for the part of its brain that processed fear had been cauterised. A horse like this would never shy or refuse a command, but as such it was dependent on its rider's judgement and instincts to keep them both safe in doing so.

Higher, now. The crest must be close. Cold, arid air cut into their lungs. Another jump, and a narrow track led up. Spindles of pale ice blocked the way to the other side and their descent. Verity pushed the horse forward and gave the command to jump, making it tuck its forelegs in close to the breastplate and pull back its head. Ice shattered with a sound like breaking glass, fragments bouncing from the armour and spinning away like tiny daggers. As the horse extended its forelegs for the landing, a disembodied pain lanced up from somewhere below and forward of her hand, and Verity knew the horse was injured; that a splinter of ice had found its way through the shoe's protection and into the tender frog.

The horse came down on a narrow area, momentum still carrying them forward. Verity had to calculate the next jump immediately, to a ledge thirty feet down. Upturned knives of ice sailed below. Verity fought to suppress the pain, reassuring the horse and supporting it with the strength of her own mind. Hoofs down, throwing her forward in the saddle. She recovered her balance. Another jump. There lay the track, a hundred feet below, and along it raced another rider. She'd have to plan the next jump precisely if they were to land safely and not lose ground. She found the place and directed the horse to it. The horse made the final leap straight towards their quarry, flying down parallel to the path that ran along the edge of the crater. They landed running, the man on the fleeing horse yards ahead. The surge of adrenaline and its bleedback through Verity's connection sustaining the horse against its pain a little longer. White ice and black dust raced by, each stride bringing her closer to him.

Verity focused on the spy's back and sat forward in the saddle, knees gripping. "Halt, in the name of the Meritocracy!"

The man's long, loose hair obscured his face as he crouched over his horse's neck, his body tensing. Verity realised what he was doing and dodged her own horse aside as the other pivoted and kicked out, its hoofs missing Verity's horse's ribs by six inches.

Unbalanced, Verity clutched at the reins with her left hand while her right flailed for balance over the ice rushing under the horse. Its hogged mane offered no purchase. At her thought-prompt, the horse made a short jump into the direction she was overbalancing, resettling her in the saddle and drawing them level with their quarry. "I'm armed!" Verity called out to him. "Stop and you won't be harmed!"

The man's shoulder twisted. His hand reached to something on his belt; a weapon. Verity reached to her left hip and the handle of her katana. The man's head turned at the hiss of steel. The blade rushed through the air and Verity caught only a glimpse of his expression before head and shoulders parted company and his face disappeared in a vortex of hair and blood. The horse beneath the man's body stumbled, its head went down, and its legs gave way under it. It spun out of control, into the wall of sharp ice bordering the rim of the crater, while the body of the man flew from the saddle, limbs flinging limply about it, and disappeared over the edge. The horse *screamed*.

Verity had already given the signal to her own horse to stop, and it had to swerve as the fallen horse lashed out with its feet, its flailing hoofs threatening to foul with the legs of the other and send it down too.

The fallen horse had come to a stop lying on its side, and it made no attempt to rise. Its head twisted on its neck, ears back, eyes rolled to the whites. It groaned, and a terrible broadcast of pain penetrated Verity's senses. She kicked her feet out of her stirrups and dismounted, laying her katana on the ground before going to the horse.

Blood spread rapidly on the ground beneath it, solidifying before Verity's eyes. She pulled off her helmet, feeling sweat freeze on her skin where its cheekplates had been. She cut her connection with her own her own horse with a thought-prompt, and bent over to unlatch the faceplate of the injured one's armour, revealing the gem-like implant in the centre of its forehead. Putting her hand to the neural shunt on her own forehead, she synced herself to the horse's signal.

She fell to one knee upon the ice with a sudden intake of breath. A torrent of pure agony assailed her. Verity fought against the pain to run diagnostics on the horse. *Right lung: punctured. Ribs: broken. Blood loss: 250 cm^3s^{-1}*. The damage was too severe. There was only one thing left she could offer this horse.

She pulled the gun from her belt and put finger to the trigger. Gasping and doubled over from the icy spasms convulsing through the horse, she got to her feet and pointed the gun at the implant in its head.

The gun discharged with a snap, and the horse's head fell limp. Electricity crackled briefly through the cybernetic armour, and the horse's signal and the pain that came with it went out. Verity dropped the gun and stood, bent forward, hands on knees. She closed her eyes and her breath came out as a whimpering sob. *The fool.* Why had he not stopped when she had warned him? What other outcome could he possibly have expected? Now the horse was dead as well as him because of his choice. What could it be he had taken that was worth that?

She'd have to find his head and take that back. Farron could still get whatever information he needed, provided she hurried.

"Don't move. Stand up and turn around slowly."

Verity opened her eyes. Her hunched-over shadow stretched in front of her against a trembling cone of light from a source behind. As she turned, she recognised John Aaron standing there, his armour identical to hers, and her own katana in his hand, pointed at her. Frozen blood coated its blade. Beyond him, her horse stood with its injured foot raised from the ice, and his horse a little farther back.

She had disconnected from her horse when she'd connected to the injured one to run diagnostics. She couldn't sense it or use it now. Her gun was lying on the ice at her feet.

What was he doing? She couldn't recall having had much to do with him, just that he was a new recruit who'd come in on the last transfer. Verity didn't get on particularly well with anyone on the base, but her main rivalry was with Sergeant Black, because of various things that had gone on here as well as when their paths had crossed before they'd both been transferred to Callisto. She had no such history with John Aaron, unless she'd slighted him in some way she'd neither realised nor remembered. She straightened herself and tried to keep her voice steady when she spoke.

"I'm your sergeant. That's my sword. Is there a problem?"

"You're the problem, that's what." Behind his visor his eyes burned with righteous passion, and his voice was unsteady with emotion.

Verity forced saliva into her suddenly dry mouth. It wasn't something she'd done. It was something she *was*.

"You and those infernal scientists who think they're gods. I wasn't alive to stop the four that came before you, but I've stopped *him*." His head gave a brief jerk to the path behind. "And I can stop you, and after you I'll stop however many more it takes. Destiny has decided that your life ends here and now, Zeta."

How had he found out? Verity put the question aside for now and thought quickly through what her training had given her. He had not killed her when he had the opportunity, when she stood with her back to him to deal with the horse. Even now, rather than shooting her with his gun, he seemed possessed with the irony of killing Verity with her own katana, and the blade shook from the tremor in his hand. He was inexperienced, zealous, overwhelmed with idealistic emotion. He had not her training nor experience. Words would unnerve him. Tactics could unhinge him.

"That sword's main strength is in its opponent not seeing it until it's too late." Did he hear the quaver of fear she detected in her own voice?

Aaron's eyes narrowed behind his visor. "Lofty words for one so young."

"I am the child of Caleb. I trained in Torrmede." If she could remain calm, while intimidating or angering him, it would make things easier. *An irrational mind does not fight rationally.* "I'm Pilgrennon's blood and Blake's direct descendant!"

"Pilgrennon was the devil incarnate, and Torrmede is on another world!" He raised the sword, and Verity brought up her arm, blocking the blade with the bracer protecting her forearm as it came down. She twisted into him, using the momentum of her shoulders to launch a punch into his chin, dislodging his helmet and exposing his throat. As he reeled back, Verity sensed a tremor through the ground, a shadow over her. His horse reared, hoofs kicking out for her. She grabbed hold of his armour and spun on her heel, interposing his body between herself and the horse, and the blow struck him in the chest with such force his armour made an audible crack. Verity flung him to the ground, landing with her knee on his diaphragm, and pinned down his arm, working her thumb under the fastening of his gauntlet and digging in to the tendons of his wrist until he cried out and dropped the katana.

She punched him in the jaw to dislodge his helmet fully. His skin was a bloodless white, and tears of pain welled in his eyes. Vapour left his nostrils in short, rapid breaths. Verity put her thumb to the neural shunt in his forehead, disconnecting him from his horse. Her knees trembled as she got up off him. "Iaido is the way of drawing the sword, not the way of parading about waving a sword. Now put your hands together!"

Aaron didn't comply. He struggled with his breathing for a moment, and then he coughed weakly. "I think my ribs are broken."

Verity picked up her katana and tried to wipe it on her

cloak, but the blood had frozen on it. She resheathed it, making a mental note that she needed to take it out before it had the chance to thaw. She found a climbing rope in the gear bag behind the saddle. "Put your hands together, unless you want me to put you out of your misery as I did with the horse!"

"If I don't succeed today, someone else will finish the job for me," he said, but he lifted his hands weakly and clasped them together, fingers interlocked. Verity tied his wrists. She picked up her helmet and cast about for the spy's head, sighting it some distance away, hair splayed out on the ground. She ran to it in leaping strides. The cheek had frozen to the ice and it left a graze on the skin when she pulled it up. Already the eyes had become glazed and vacant, lids drooping. He would have lost consciousness probably seconds after his head hit the ice. For how long could a brain be subjected to ischaemia before permanent damage started to occur? She remembered learning something like that in Torrmede. It seemed a long time gone. She put the question to the research base's ANT, through its radio mast somewhere behind the ice spire. It retrieved the data from its banks almost immediately: four minutes maximum, assuming optimum reperfusion.

Arrays of Neurotechnology could retrieve information for her, or run probability computations, but they couldn't make decisions. She would have to choose what was best. Killing him had not been the ideal outcome, but running through what had happened again as she strode back to John Aaron, still she saw no alternative. She'd told him to stop, twice. He'd reached for a weapon. It had been her or him.

Aaron whimpered like a child when she tore his cloak off him. Turning to a stand of ice spikes, she raised her knee to her chest and brought her heel down hard into the heart of the formation, smashing it. She gathered the shards into the cloak, placed the head in the centre, and folded the cloth around it to form an ice pack. Incorrect freezing damaged cells, but she hoped the ice would only chill the brain, with bone and skin insulating it.

Her horse stood with its right front hoof lifted slightly. Aaron's horse was uninjured and would be faster. Verity synced herself to it. She put the cloak with the man's head in it in the bag behind the saddle. She would never reach the base on time if she had to lead the injured horse. Leaving the horse here in a sweat where it would freeze to death would be irresponsible, and she supposed, so was abandoning Aaron to the same fate, even if his actions made him a criminal.

"Stand up and come over here!" Verity moved to the injured horse and reached across to take hold of its bridle.

Aaron's mouth distorted with pain as he struggled to his feet, a tear dribbling from his eye and freezing as it tracked down his face.

He came forward, holding up his clasped and bound hands as though praying to whatever deity he believed in that made Verity's heritage so objectionable to him. Verity lashed his wrists to the pommel of the horse's saddle.

"Get on and return this horse to the base. Let them deal with you there when it's done."

He got into the saddle as Verity returned to the other horse. "But I'm not synced to this horse. I can't ride it with no interface on this terrain."

"Then learn to, like people did in the old days, or fall and die." As she adjusted the stirrups, Verity glanced at the dead horse's bulk and the sheet of frozen blood under it. "Noble death is for the noble."

She jumped up, caught the front and back of the saddle, and swung her leg over. The horses were all eighteen hands high, and she'd never have mounted them on Earth without standing on something.

Behind her, Aaron shouted, "Waste of time expecting compassion from something made by man and not God! You don't have a soul."

Verity turned her horse and set off back along the track

around the spire. She urged the horse to as fast a gallop as she dared on this narrow path with sharp ice debris bordering its edges. For what seemed like an age they weaved along the path, concentrating so fiercely it felt dangerous even to risk an instant to blink. At last the shard-like outcrops of ice dwindled, and the treacherous terrain of the eruptions around the newer crater gave way to the older dark plain of the great Valhalla crater with its knobbly spires blunted by erosion. The horse galloped flat out towards the research base on the horizon. Verity counted seconds.

The gates and the walls of the compound loomed ahead. Verity rode straight through the courtyard and into the stables. Hoofs thundered on the flooring in the main corridor. A bespectacled man stood ahead of her, a hold-all in each hand. He was young, tall, and slight, with a sickly demeanor and an expression suggesting he was about to throw up.

"Get out of my way!" Verity drove the horse into the man's shoulder, knocking him against the wall. She didn't look back. She would have known had the horse stepped on the man, and it was his fault for causing an obstruction.

A woman in a lab coat met her at the corridor junction. "Take this to Inquisitor Farron, at once!" Verity pulled the head in the cloak out of the bag and slung it at her. The woman turned and ran with it down the corridor towards the laboratories.

Her connection with the ANT told her the four minutes was up. The brain should still be in reasonable enough condition for Farron to get the information from it, whatever information that was. Perhaps he would also find why the spy had been prepared to lose his own life and kill a perfectly good horse over it. Now the race was over, her breathing came loud and fast in the corridor, and the heaving of the animal's ribs pushed her feet out with each breath.

An uncomfortable tension knotted her stomach, refusing to be reasoned away. Aaron's words returned to her: *If I don't succeed today, someone else will finish the job for me.* What did that mean? Was it something to do with the spy? Could he have been involved too? Could it be that a conspiracy was afoot, and some unknown number of people on this base plotted against Verity, just because of the way she had been born? She queried the ANT for John Aaron's location and it came back negative. He shouldn't be out of range. There were various black spots on the scarp where the line of sight to the mast was blocked, but he must off the scarp by now, so where was he? There was no record on the ANT's database of any thought-prompts having been received from him since she'd left him, and the ANT's scanning equipment could not locate him or the horse anywhere within its range.

Why had the spy not surrendered? What secret was so vital it could be worth dying over? Verity was tired, and she would have liked to have seen Farron and found out if the data in the man's brain had survived and could be extracted, but attending to the horse took priority. She flicked her feet out of the stirrups and slid off. Leading the horse by the bridle, she headed back towards the stable block.

It was times like this she missed Gecko most. His name was Lieutenant Dwayne Uxbridge, but everyone called him Gecko, after some incident in his past of which Verity had never discovered the full details. Probably it was to do with his controlled, patient manner, what his squadron members called cold bloodedness. Verity had always suspected that whole squadron laughed at her behind her back. They seemed to find endless amusement in the phenomenon of someone like Gecko carrying on with the likes of her.

There had never been any expectation from either of them for it to last; it never did in the Sky Forces. Her area of expertise had been in animal handling, so after she'd been promoted to sergeant, she'd been relocated to the new base on Callisto. Gecko's specialism was machines, and the Dennis Terraforming Company was paying him to oversee a survey of one of Saturn's moons.

She stroked the horse's neck, now wet with thawed sweat and condensation as they passed through the stable doors.

Since they'd parted, Verity had come to miss Gecko's great tolerance for being shouted at; an ability to sit calmly and humor her while she raged and lost her temper at him over something that always seemed trivial afterwards. Other people, it seemed, so easily took umbrage over a harsh word or an abrupt comment, but not Gecko.

Verity wanted to send word to him, to tell him what had happened here. Perhaps he could give some words of reassurance that would make what had happened feel less of a shock. She had already sent him two messages in the three months she'd been on Callisto, but he'd replied to neither. She sometimes worried about something having befallen him out there on Titan, but more often she feared he had simply moved on from the past, and his refusal to contact her was merely a hint to her to do the same.

chapter two

ANOTHER HORSE POKED ITS HEAD over a door as Verity led hers into the stables. Its nostrils flared and its upper lip pulled back over its teeth, and as it exhaled a great moist gust into Verity's face, she sensed an urge and a broadcast of frustration. It was a male horse, a stallion. The other horses were all mares, although Verity never really thought about that when she worked with them. The stallion must have been brought in on the recent shuttle.

The ANT still returned negative when she requested the whereabouts of Private Aaron. What if he hadn't gone back to the base as she had ordered him, but had gone somewhere else? It had already occurred to her he might have something to do with the spy, and the spy must have been going somewhere, and what if Aaron had known about it and had gone there? Perhaps she had made the wrong decision. Verity made a request through the ANT to Commodore Smith, asking to speak with him as soon as possible.

She led the horse past the stallion and into its loose box, and then divested herself of her helmet and sweaty jacket and gloves. The horse nudged a panel at the back of the stall and water poured into the bucket fixed there. Verity quickly got the bridle off so the horse could drink freely. She soon had the saddle and the rest of the armour off, and hung them on the door to the stall. The ice on the horse's coat had already melted, leaving the hair damp, so she rubbed vigorously with a stable blanket, to dry the horse off and stimulate its circulation. She checked the diagnostics from the connection: horse was uninjured, heart rate and breathing slightly increased from the exercise, and horse was *happy* from being home and having its armour off and being rubbed down.

Verity selected a spanner from their place on the wall ledge outside the stalls, and gave the command for the horse to pick up its foot. They always liked it when their shoes were taken off. As she cradled the hoof in her hand and bent over, something in the horse's vision caught her attention. She put down the foot and looked up to see a young man enter — the same one her horse had knocked into in the corridor.

"Hi," he said, nervously.

Had he come in here looking for an apology? Verity wasn't about to apologise to him; she was on an important mission and he should have got out the way. In the horse's vision his skin looked greenish, because horses can't see the red end of the spectrum, but even in Verity's own eyesight he looked sickly and nauseous. "I'm busy." She turned back to the horse, but its eyesight confirmed he was still standing there, watching her. Couldn't he take a hint? Didn't he have work to do, like everyone else on this base?

"It's Zeta, isn't it?"

The memory of Aaron's words outside flashed before Verity. Aaron, who was still unaccounted for, and was responsible of this nervous discomfort in her. How did this man know that? Who was he, and what was he doing here? Her hand wandered to the hilt of her katana. "Don't call me that!" The ears of every horse in the stable block turned back, hoofs stamped, and Verity's horse let out a whinny. "No-one calls me that! You understand?"

"I- I'm sorry... I looked you up in the staff directory, I was told you were the person I needed to speak to... I understood that was your name."

"My name's Sergeant Verity!" Verity's hand still rested on her katana, but the slight pressure of her fingers brought back not the slight movement of steel in the sheath, but a sticky, viscous resistance. Too late she remembered the blood. "*Shite!*" She would have to deal with that later. Verity tried to control her temper, transmitting soothing thoughts to the horse, which snorted and moved uneasily as she lifted its foot to remove the shoe.

The man flinched at the expletive. "I was told you were the best person to approach on the matter of the horses. My name's Vladimir Bolokhovski." It was only after speaking a longer sentence like this that Verity noticed his slight accent.

"Look, I've told you I'm busy. If you're a civilian, you're not supposed to be in the stable block at any rate." Verity wished he would go away. She knew her unease was affecting the horses, and he was making it worse. She unlocked the bolts securing the shoe to the bone implants and separated the inner cushion from the thick protective outer, its surface scalloped for grip and patterned with the holes of the retracted crampons. "You need to see Commodore Smith if you need access to the horses."

"I already did. He told me to speak to you."

Verity looked over her shoulder at him, narrowing her eyes as she stroked the powerful black neck of the horse. "What for? He knows I'm busy." She ducked under the horse's neck and went between it and the wall to take the shoes off the other side.

Vladimir put his hands on his knees and craned his neck forward, trying to look under the horse at her. "I'm writing a thesis," he said.

Verity grimaced. Was he trying to impress her? "What's that make you, a Not-Properly-a-Doctor?"

"I'm working in the research group of Professor Eglin at Torrmede."

"Torrmede? Didn't think they let Russians into Torrmede."

"I'm half British. And Torrmede doesn't discriminate. They'll let in anyone with the grades."

"What did you study there? Spying, poisoning, or nuclear weapons?"

The horse's vision showed Vladimir straighten up and make a distasteful face. "Russia hasn't been communist since

1991, and we're starting to adopt meritocratic rule."

"Starting?"

"We have public referenda on many political decisions. A democratically elected government still makes some of them, but we're gradually moving towards meritocratic autonomy."

Verity scowled. "No country under the yoke of *politicians* can be called a meritocracy. If your country was worth the soil it was made of, its electorate would make all its decisions."

"Hmm, wise words," said Vladimir quietly, "yet I'd say that wisdom was beyond your years, and I recall once reading something attributing a very similar comment to Jananin Blake."

Verity squeezed between the horse's rump and the wall with the shoes in her hands. "Well, I think I can be forgiven for stealing Blake's words. After all, she *was* Blake."

As the horse pawed the ground, enjoying the light weight of its feet and the sensation of the layer of warm sand on the floor, Verity put the shoes in the storage rack opposite and hefted up the saddle. The metal edge on the outer part of one of the stirrups caught the light, sending a bright rectangle of reflection flitting about the roof of the stalls. The stallion's eyes rolled. His nostrils flared and he backed away from the stable door with a snort.

Verity stared at the stallion. "He's afraid. He's not fearless?" She dumped the saddle on the rack.

"You don't mix testosterone with fearlessness."

Apparently satisfied that the threat posed by shiny things was gone, the stallion stretched his neck over the door of his stall to smell Vladimir. The man took a nervous step out the way. He didn't look like he'd seen very much in the way of either horses or testosterone.

"What do you know about it?" Verity scowled.

"That's what my thesis is about." He raised his voice at the end of the statement, making it sound like a question. "I'm doing a doctorate in genetic engineering. I engineered this horse."

"Oh," said Verity after a pause in which things started to make sense. "Well, congratulations. He's a nice animal. Apart from being frightened of tack."

"That's why I need to talk to you. There's supposed to be a breeding programme commencing at this base."

Verity picked up her armour, closed the stable door, and reached up to the implant on her forehead, cutting her connection to the horse. "These are working horses, not breeding stock." Horses were for riding, and they couldn't be ridden if they were pregnant. But at the same time, a frisson of excitement stirred in her. Foals. She'd never seen a foal in real life, only in videos and textbook pictures.

"The company that owns them have decided they want to breed them as well, and that's why I've been sent."

"You're going to have to speak to me later. I have a meeting with the Commodore."

In her billet, Verity threw the armour on the bed and examined the katana, swearing at the blood smeared up the blade and inside the sheath. She filled the sheath with water and left it propped up in the shower, before wiping the blade carefully and polishing it. She laid it down on the floor close to the wall before stripping off the rest of her armour and throwing that on the bed, and pulling on the charcoal boilersuit that was standard indoor dress on the Callisto base.

She exited her quarters and walked straight into the Commodore.

"Ah, Sergeant Verity. I understand you want to speak to me?"

"Yes, Commodore, Sir." Verity stepped back from him in a hurry. "There's been an incident involving Private Aaron. I think he might have absconded."

Verity had never seen Commodore Smith smile, but he raised his eyebrows and turned his dark brown eyes to her. "I had a quick read through the ANT's details on the matter. Let's discuss this in my office."

In the Commodore's office, Verity took a seat on the outside of the desk. "Well," said Commodore Smith, sitting. "Can you go through what happened? I'm going to need your account for the report."

Verity hesitated; if she had made a bad decision, she could be court-martialled. She carefully explained the horse chase, how she had shouted twice for the spy to stop, how he'd reached for a weapon, and how she'd beheaded him, how Aaron had got hold of her katana — and at this point, she noticed the Commodore cast his eyes down to her belt to check she didn't have it — and how she had overcome him but sent him back with the horse because of the necessity to get the spy's head back as quickly as possible.

Smith frowned, fingering his upper lip. "Did he say anything when he attacked you?"

"Uh," said Verity. She didn't have to tell him the exact circumstances of her birth; the Meritocracy made that information private from employers, so that people with powerful relatives couldn't exploit their connections. "He'd found out someone who was my ancestor had done something he didn't agree with. He thought killing me would avenge a crime he thought had been committed against him."

The Commodore's frown deepened. "Sounds like he was mentally disturbed. That should have showed up in his screening."

"Do you know where he might have gone, Sir?" Anxiety was creeping back into Verity's stomach.

"If he's not back, I don't know what's happened to him. The ANT can't find him, so he mustn't have left the scarp. It's quite probable he could have fallen off the horse and killed himself, with no interface. Perhaps even deliberately knowing he'd failed and dishonoured himself."

"I doubt it," said Verity, thinking privately that John Aaron didn't have any honour. "You don't think he could have gone anywhere?"

He shrugged. "Where?"

She considered. "There's no proper GPS for getting detailed surveillance beyond the base. He could have had an ally put a ship down. The spy took the horse and he was going somewhere. He was a spy who presumably got his information from someone. It might be John Aaron was an inside informant."

Smith shook his head. "Unlikely. But it bears consideration. I've no idea how the spy got in here. The ANT reported unauthorised personnel, but we recently had a shipment of goods and a staff change, so it's most likely he found a way to stow away on that. It is an awfully long way to come to Callisto to steal something, and rather expensive using one's own transport. Possibly the spy panicked when the alarm went off, and took a horse in some kind of desperate hope, thinking he might be able to hide outside."

Verity thought that seemed a bit of a stupid thing for a spy to do, but then she also thought it was stupid of him to have reached for a weapon when she had told him twice to stop. It could be he was merely a very inept spy. She said nothing.

"I'll need to speak to Inquisitor Farron about the spy." The Commodore's face gave a slight twitch when he spoke Farron's name, and his voice changed tone slightly. "It makes sense to ask him if he knows anything about Private Aaron while we're there, but before we go, there's another matter I need to discuss with you. There's a breeding programme commencing involving the base's horses. Torrmede have sent someone to oversee it, some sort of scientist."

"Vladimir Bolokhovski." Verity pulled the name off the

ANT. "He was hanging around the stable block earlier."

"Yes. I'd like you to introduce him to the facilities here, and make sure he knows what he's doing with this breeding programme."

"But Sir," she said, "it's Referendum Day! I'm supposed to get the afternoon off so I can read and vote."

"Sergeant Verity, I am not suggesting you have to do it this afternoon. I meant for you to arrange with him to do it in your own time."

Verity protested, "I'm looking after the core-sampling project already! Sergeant Black's better at this sort of thing than I am; she harps on about it enough. Why don't you ask her to do it?" Verity frowned. "Has Sergeant Black been saying things about me?"

"Verity, we are not discussing Sergeant Black's profile of abilities, we are discussing yours. I'm aware you have recently been involved in an incident, but may I remind you that you are a sergeant in the Sky Forces, and while this particular branch of the Sky Forces is not a true military division, you are still expected to conduct yourself in the proper manner."

Something in Smith's expression told Verity her suspicion was correct. Sergeant Black had never liked Verity, since even before Callisto. When she'd confided it in Gecko, he'd thought it was because Verity was younger than Black, and Black envied her Magnolia Order connection. Her enmity had got worse when Verity had been promoted to Sergeant only a month after Black, who was five years Verity's senior. Furiously, Verity wondered why, if Black had a problem with her, she couldn't say it to her face.

"Do you think it is acceptable, just because certain aspects of your career profile are very strong, that you should neglect other parts of it?"

Verity folded her arms. "I don't know what you mean."

"Don't be disingenuous! You weren't promoted to sergeant for nothing, but it certainly wasn't your interpersonal skills that put you in line for it. Now, if you are at all concerned about what I am going to write on my report about this incident, you can put those concerns out of your mind now. I'm convinced you acted in a manner that was absolutely judicious and rational, and your training has served you extremely well today. Had you contacted me through the ANT and asked me what to do, I would have told you to do exactly as you did. Only you didn't, quite rightly, because you knew explaining the situation to me would cost you time you needed, and so you made the decisions yourself, and they were the right ones."

Smith paused to give Verity some time to consider this before continuing. "Now, your most recent appraisal shows that your interpersonal skills need work. This is one of two reasons why I've decided to give this duty to you. If you want to know my other reason, it's because I honestly think you are the best member of staff here in terms of handling the horses. Certainly Sergeant Black and I are trained to use them, and do so effectively, but you *understand* them. Surely you can see that the best person to train someone how to handle horses is such a person, who understands them thus?"

Verity looked away from his face and stared at the surface of the desk. "I suppose so, Sir."

"Good, then. Let's go to the Inquisitor's laboratory."

*

The Inquisitor greeted them in the entrance to his laboratory. Lloyd Farron had wavy hair with a tawny auburn colour, extending into luxuriant full-length sideburns. With his sturdy, medium-height build, he looked like a lion. He had a mug of tea in one hand and a chocolate biscuit in the other.

"Morning, Commodore. Sergeant Verity." Lloyd glanced sideways at Verity and smiled, one eyebrow twisting below his interface apparatus. In addition to the standard fixed neural shunt in the centre of the forehead, the Inquisitor had two auxiliary shunts just forward of his temples with a web of diodes and extra wiring interconnecting all three, supposedly to shield his mind from bleedback off the people he interrogated. Verity doubted the efficacy of those, and there had to be some truth somewhere at the root of the rumour of the inquisitors' compromised sanity. No-one can dodge bleedback, same as you can't evade age and death. A hundred years ago people used to say 'death and taxes', but that no longer worked since the Meritocracy made paying taxes an optional privilege. Perhaps one day scientists would find a cure for ageing, and then there'd only be bleedback and death left. Verity couldn't see death ever going away; probability always wins in the end.

"Indeed it is morning!" realised Commodore Smith, his attention drawn to the windows running the span of the outer wall, where the sun glowed on the horizon.

"For the next four days," said Verity.

Lloyd rubbed his hands together briskly. "Good Referendum Day! Was there something you wanted to speak to me about?" He glanced rapidly back and forth between Verity and the Commodore.

"Yes." Smith fidgeted with his fingers. Tall and sable haired, he looked very different to Lloyd. Verity could see the discomfort written on his face. People feared a man like Lloyd Farron, who could prise open someone's mind at will. Verity, on the other hand, had from her first encounter with him seen it as something exciting; dangerously exhilarating.

"I'll need your report on the spy Verity terminated," Smith said.

"I don't have the information yet. It shouldn't take more than a day, and I'll file a private report on the ANT once I'm sure I've extracted everything."

Verity had been looking round the lab while they spoke, at the computers and the interrogation chair with its thick straps to restrain the arms and heads of Lloyd Farron's victims. In the far corner a lot of machinery had been connected to something that Verity realised, with a pang of dread, was the head of the spy she had brought back, mounted on a stick like some grisly trophy. The long hair had been hacked off with scissors, and the face was covered with lacerations from Verity's makeshift ice pack. The wound at the neck she had made with her katana looked unnaturally straight, perfectly horizontal, and thick tubes delivering oxygenated reanimation fluid had been clamped to its blood vessels. Wires trailed over the table around the head, and jacks had been plugged into the shunt on its forehead. Saliva dribbled constantly from the mouth, and the left eye was a mess of clotted blood where a shard of ice had punctured it. The right eye swivelled, looked directly at her, and a chill prickling crawled from her scalp right the way down to the backs of her knees. She'd done that... he'd made her do that. Why hadn't he stopped when she'd told him?

The Commodore must have noticed the shift in her attention, for a slight noise of disgust escaped him. Verity turned to see him staring at the head. "You're not going to leave him like *that*, are you?"

"No," said the Inquisitor, dipping his biscuit in his tea. "He'll be put out of his misery once he divulges the information I need from him." The biscuit broke as he lifted his hand, and plopped into the tea. He made a distasteful face at the stub between his finger and thumb.

The Commodore took a deep breath and straightened his belt. "You see that you do your job and make him. He may be a spy, but... *well.*"

Verity stared at the head. Yes, he'd been a spy. She needed to rise above pitying him, thinking of him as a man, even, because he was a traitor to the Meritocracy, and this was what people who plotted to bring down the Meritocracy deserved.

Commodore Smith cleared his throat and looked conspicuously away from the head. "Do you know anything of

Private John Aaron? I don't know if you will know the name. If you've seen him about before, have you ever picked up any... *vibes* from him?"

"Hmm, Aaron." The Inquisitor dipped another biscuit in his tea and put it in his mouth. He frowned as he chewed, turning away slightly and putting his fingers to his interface. "I think I know the one you mean. He had something he didn't want others to know. He was very... assured in his convictions on a particular matter, although I'm not sure what it was."

"That would fit. It turns out he's some kind of nutcase. He just made an attempt on Verity's life, and now he's AWOL."

"Hmm," said the Inquisitor again. He glanced up at Verity. "Didn't hurt you, did he?"

Verity shook her head. Lloyd suddenly grinned. "Didn't think he could. Ah well, *absit omen*."

"Well, if you have any information, please put it on the ANT." The Commodore was turning to leave. Something in his manner betrayed an eagerness to be elsewhere. He didn't like the Inquisitor.

After Smith had left, Lloyd said, "Who was that man you were speaking with, in the stables, Verity? Did he come in on the last landing?"

"He is a Nearly-A-Doctor who sires horses," said Verity.

Lloyd roared with laughter. He offered her his tin of chocolate biscuits. Verity didn't want to eat in front of the spy's head, so she put one in her pocket. "How do you mean?" Lloyd asked.

"He says he's training to be a genetic engineer."

"Hmm," said Lloyd, tapping his signet ring against his tea mug. It was an odd design, titanium with alternating bands of anodised violet.

"Lloyd," said Verity, admiring the strong shape of his brow and nose and his broad shoulders. She never could think of what to say to him on that front. It wasn't that he was older, because he couldn't be more than ten years her senior, but because he seemed so much more *mature*. It always felt inappropriate somehow. "When you get the data off the spy, I know you can't tell me what it is, but if there's anything I need to know…" Verity found her attention once more drawn to the head on the bench, where it watched her with an eye that looked somehow furious. "You will tell me? There's something going on here. Something to do with John Aaron. I tried to tell the Commodore, but I don't think he really understood."

She didn't want to reveal any more of what she was thinking in front of the spy's head. She knew he couldn't speak, but he could still hear.

"Of course," said Lloyd.

*

In the refectory she found Vladimir, sitting at a table by himself.

She sat unceremoniously on a chair opposite him. "The Commodore says I've to help you."

"Thanks." said Vladimir. "I think."

Verity ripped open the top of her carton of food and stuck her spoon in. "I'll show you the exercise centrifuge tomorrow. We can't use it this afternoon because it's Referendum Day today."

Vladimir made a face. "I don't care about things like that. There's work and more important things to be getting on with."

Verity stared at him across the table. He had a very fair complexion, with light brown hair and eyes of that genuine blue colour resulting from no iris pigmentation. Perhaps he might be considered conventionally attractive, if she'd been bothered to care about such things. "Right. Well, if you don't exercise here, you'll waste away in the low gravity. And you'll have to exercise your horse, too. I've never put a horse that's not fearless in a centrifuge before. Should be interesting at any rate."

Vladimir looked alarmed. "I have to handle him? There's not staff here trained in it?"

"The staff here look after the working horses here. He's your project. You look after him."

He looked out the panoramic window at the sun on the horizon and Jupiter in the sky. "When you say tomorrow, do you mean 24 hours-ish from now, or the next time the sun rises?"

"I mean Terran standard time."

"It might have to wait longer than that. I think I caught some sort of cold on the transport ship, and now I don't feel at all well."

"It's like snot and crap and you feel like shit?" Verity stirred her food. "It's a reaction to no gravity. All the fluid in your lungs and your sinuses comes out of place and it feels like a cold. The other thing's breathlessness and feeling tired? That's because the air out here is less oxygenated. It's like high altitude air when you go up Olympus Mons."

"I've never been up Olympus Mons," said Vladimir nervously. He stirred his soup, looking away from Verity in an embarrassed sort of way. When he finally put his spoon in his mouth, his face crumpled up. "This soup is awful! It's like something I'd use in the lab! What is this stuff?" Vladimir rotated the container in his hands and frowned as he read the label printed on the white carton in plain black font. "*Levigated esculents*? It even *sounds* like something that belongs in a lab!"

"It's made out of genetically modified plants grown on sewage," said Verity.

"Tastes it."

"We have to have sustainable food. It would cost a fortune to keep shipping in proper food from Earth or Mars. Well, although they make an exception for the Inquisitor. He gets tea and complimentary biscuits." Verity remembered the biscuits and put her hand in her pocket to find it full of melted chocolate. She held up her hand, spreading brown-smeared fingers. Vladimir grimaced.

"Don't you ever miss proper food?" he asked as Verity licked her hand.

"What, like bloody steaks, and sheep's hearts, and liver? I miss those."

Vladimir shrugged. "The kebabs on Mars are the best. Don't think they deliver out here, 'though."

Verity hadn't expected him to say that. He looked like the sort of person who didn't eat meat. "Kebabs aren't *proper* meat. It's just processed rubbish."

Vladimir said casually, "What other animals have you eaten — I mean, worked with? Besides horses."

Verity tilted her food carton and scraped the remainder into her spoon. "Birds."

"Birds?"

"Hawks. The Meritocracy uses them for surveillance. They can see in much more detail than people or computers can, and they're tetrachromats, so they can see into the ultraviolet region."

Vladimir tore his bread open and poked at a packet of synthetic butter with his knife. "What things are ultraviolet?"

"Stuff like flowers. People's hair and fingernails, that greasy area on people's foreheads and noses. Urine."

"Urine?"

"When buzzards and things are flying around, they can see places rodents have piddled. That's how they know where to look."

"What does ultraviolet look like?"

"I dunno." Verity shrugged. "Can't explain it."

Vladimir frowned. "Does it look like blue?"

"No. It sort of merges into it though. Like how green merges into blue going the other way. You see it with the bird's eyes, not your own. I can't explain it in terms of how humans see, same as you can't explain to a horse what red looks like."

"Are hawks better than horses to interface with, then?"

Verity sniffed. "When they first give you it, you think it's really ace, but after you've had it for a bit, you realise it doesn't do anything else, and you can't really train it much. All you can do is tell it where to go and analyse what it sees. Dogs are kind of annoying too."

Vladimir's expression lightened. "I like dogs."

Gecko liked dogs, too. He'd had an enormous German Shepherd bitch, who had gone with him everywhere he'd been allowed to take her. She'd always slept on his bed and made his billet smell of dog.

"Thing with dogs is, they think disgusting things are appetising. And then you're always having to factor in smells. If you're working with dogs and something smells, it hijacks their attention and they won't stop thinking about it, and the worst thing is you get bleedback."

"Bleedback?"

"The dogs' impatience and distractedness get transmitted to you through the interface." Verity tapped the implant on her forehead. "One time a fox or something had shat in the grass and the dog I was handling smelled it and tried to eat it, and for a moment I felt like I wanted to eat it, too. Bleedback off dogs is the pits."

Vladimir grimaced again and touched his own implant.

"And then there were cephalopods," Verity said. "They were experimental. Didn't work so well."

"Cephalopods? How don't they work?"

"They might work, eventually. They're useful underwater because they're intelligent and dextrous." Verity opened and closed her fingers in a way suggesting tentacles. "I think it was just because they're so different to us in terms of how their brains work. They're a long way from us on those evolutionary diagrams biologists do."

"They're a different *phylum*."

Verity frowned. "Whatever that means." She drained her glass of water, and rose. Vladimir pushed back his chair and stood too.

"I suppose I'll see you tomorrow, then." He followed Verity as she headed for the main doors.

"At the centrifuge, at eight."

Sheets of paper and graffiti covered the wall of the mezzanine. One poster showed a holograph of a middle-aged man with spectacles and a ginger beard. That was Sidney Worrall, formerly something in finance and currently a Spokesman for the Meritocracy. Verity took a marker pen out of her pocket and drew balls and a phallus on Sidney Worrall's forehead.

"That's not very constructive," said Vladimir.

"It's a public expression space," Verity replied. "Anyone can write what they like on it. I guess you don't have those in Russia."

Vladimir raised his palms and made an exasperated face. "You have the liberty of free speech, and you abuse it, doing things like that? In some countries, they don't have that privilege."

"His opinions stink."

"Whatever happened to defending to the death his right to say them?" Vladimir sighed. He held out his hand. "Can I borrow your pen?"

"Not if you're going to use it to write Sidney Worrall's opinions."

"I'm not, I'm going to write my own opinions."

Verity put the marker in his hand. He snapped off the cap, and wrote 'More funding for horse genetic engineers' on Sidney Worrall's lapel, and then continued to write something else in small letters on the man's jacket.

"I'm not standing about while you write War and Peace. I'm going to vote. You can gimme my pen back tomorrow." Verity went to the door,shouting over her shoulder as she left the room, "In Soviet Russia, wall writes on you!"

*

Back in her quarters, Verity took up her seat at her computer and began to look through the points of law and regulations that had been nominated for referendum by the Electorate. About a month after she'd arrived on Callisto, the moon had been declared an official province, and with the base having only a few hundred inhabitants that surely made it the smallest province in the entire Meritocracy. It also meant its electorate was entitled to nominate and cast prerogative votes on matters that only affected Callisto and its denizens. One of the first such matters to be nominated and voted in was that Referendum Day on Callisto would be the afternoon of the 24-hour day on which the sun rose.

Referendum Day this time round didn't coincide with the Meritocracy's universal referenda, which occurred once every Martian month, so there were only these provincial prerogative votes and nominations to be dealt with. As a tier two meritocrat, Verity was entitled to nominate two matters per referendum day, and to cast votes with a weighting of two on each of the nominations with the highest vote from the previous referendum day.

She had already decided to nominate a review of the exercise centrifuges at the facility, with the intention of voting for more centrifuges to be built for the horses if that nomination was then popular enough to go to referendum the next time, so she did that first, using both of her nominations on the same issue because she saw it as being more pressing than any other issues she could come up with.

After submitting her nominations to the ANT, Verity turned her attention to the nominations from last referendum day that had been brought forward to today's referendum. There were four of them: on frequency and allocation of radiocommunications access, about possibly improving the quality of the food, about regulations for importing animals as pets, and, as usual, about division of the resources of the base's one and only ANT between the Sky Forces and the scientific personnel. In addition to this, each of the thirty Spokesmen for the Meritocracy — people chosen directly by the Electorate each year, supposedly for their balanced opinions and clear judgement to act in case of emergency on behalf of the Electorate — had written a statement on the prerogative issues for Callisto, explaining their opinions on the nominations and links to statistics and reading material to back up the opinions. Whereas there was nothing to stop anyone from simply casting a vote without bothering to do any research, it was generally encouraged and thought responsible to read the letters from the Spokesmen and try to make one's vote from as balanced a perspective as possible.

Verity first opened the letter from Spokesman Julia Tindall. Tindall had been a zoologist before becoming a Spokesman, and she was always the first person Verity would vote for on the universal Spokesman referendum each year. It began with a salutation to the electorate of the province of Callisto, and as Verity had expected, the first comment on her letter was about the nomination for pets. She urged caution about bringing species to Callisto whose tolerance for low gravity had not been tested, as subjecting an animal to an environment it could not healthily cope with was inhumane. Tindall recommended that voters choose the option to allow species of pets not considered dangerous and known to be able to tolerate exposure to low gravity.

Verity read through the other comments and looked at some of the references. She read Sidney Worrall's letter with disdain, and then set about reading the other twenty-eight.

chapter three

VERITY CAME AWAKE WITH A START, heart pounding and sweat plastering her bedcover to her skin. She at once moved her hand to grasp the hard, cool shape of her wakizashi where it lay on the mattress, pressing it against her abdomen and clutching its familiar solidity with both hands. The sequence with John Aaron and the horse had played out in her dreams, only this time, she had not moved fast enough when the shadow fell over her, and it had been her ribs cracking under the blow of hoofs, and she who had fallen to the ice, and he who had stood over her with her own sword, the desperate climax of the dream bursting through into consciousness as the bloodied steel rushed through the air for its *coup de grace*.

Against the shaking thump of her pulse, she tried to reassure herself that it had been her training that had saved her life. Yet as her fingers squeezed the leather weave of the knife's handle grip, it seemed more the result of chance and blind fortune.

Verity sat up, the sweat on her body cold against the air. She hugged the covers around herself and tucked her chin down against her chest, breathing deeply as she checked the time from the ANT. She needed to be in the centrifuge to train that genetic engineer in two hours. There was little point in trying to go back to sleep now.

It had been the same the first time Verity had seen a corpse, back when she had started with the Sky Forces on Mars. The memory of it had invaded her sleep for several nights afterwards. Then it had happened a year or so later, after a particularly horrible accident. Verity and another soldier had been chasing a thief off a gyromag, and the fool in his desperation to escape had fallen from the gantry and struck a pylon on the way down, ripping his abdomen open. When she shut her eyes sometimes, she could still see the mortal horror on his face just before the moment life slipped away, and see and smell his viscera strewn across the concourse.

She gave the thought-prompt for the lights, telling herself it was a normal reaction to trauma, and that it would pass in time. With the lights on, her quarters looked bland and unthreatening. There were no shadows here to play havoc with her peripheral vision.

She'd meant not to contact Gecko again. He'd not replied to her last two messages. Perhaps this was a moment of weakness she'd regret later, but she needed him, and so she decided to give it one last try. Verity got up, still with the bedcover wrapped around herself, and switched on her computer. She left the camera off and used the microphone to record a message.

"Hi, Gecko. It's Verity. I just want to know you're okay. Send me a message. I hope Titan's going well." She paused, swallowed. "'Cause weird shit's going down here on Callisto."

She stopped the recording, marked the message as being for Lieutenant Uxbridge of Titan, and sent it to the transmissions queue.

*

Vladimir came shuffling into the centrifuge room, in the same attitude of most newcomers to a low-gravity moon, looking as though he feared he would crash into the ceiling if he put any effort into his stride. He had on a yellow T-shirt and knee-length khaki shorts with trainers and socks that came up to just below his knees.

"I said eight!"

Vladimir looked at his watch. "It's five minutes past!"

"You're still late," said Verity. "Don't they give you standard issue clothes?"

Vladimir shrugged. "Who're they?"

"I dunno. The base? Professor Whatsisface from Torrmede or whoever it was that sent you here?"

"No. In my country, people have free choice about what clothes they wear."

"In your case, free choice is a liability too far. At least get some trousers off the equipment officer. You look like an overgrown space scout." Verity held out her hand. "Pen?"

Vladimir glared at her as he dug in his pocket for it, and handed it over.

Verity let him stare around the room for a bit, composing her introduction in her head before beginning. "There are three centrifuges here. Two are for exercising horses in, and the other is for staff to use." She indicated the centrifuges with her hand, the entrances to the larger two on one side closed off, the panels above them lit in red. "Sergeant Black and Private Ferguson are using the horse centrifuges for the next hour, so we can use the staff one first to give you an idea of it."

Verity stepped up to the door of the personnel centrifuge and the green light above it. "You're not permitted to take more than five people into a centrifuge, or two people and one horse. You're not allowed to piss and shit in the centrifuges."

Vladimir glanced sharply at her.

Verity rolled her eyes. "I mean you're not allowed for your horse to do it." She bent her knee and ducked through the hatch. Inside the drum, five chairs with seatbelts lay with their backs welded to the floor, their stems riveted to the outward-slanted wall stretching all the way around and covered with grooved non-slip synthetic rubber. The light came from white panels running around the edges of the ceiling and floor. Various pieces of exercise equipment were bolted to the walls.

When Vladimir had climbed in, Verity pointed to the hatch. "To close the door, you need to press here. You do it," she added when he remained standing there watching her.

When Vladimir had pressed the button to close the door and tightened the wheel that locked it, the bar above the panel on the floor between the chairs turned green. Verity sat on a chair beside it, lying on her back and bending her knees so her legs fitted into the seat. "Everyone needs to be in a seat before you start or stop the centrifuge," she explained as she fastened the seatbelt. She checked to make sure his seatbelt was on. "When you're ready, press start."

Vladimir reached across from his seat and pressed the button. A klaxon sounded, muffled from outside the centrifuge, and the faint sound of the motor began. As the motor's pitch increased, Verity felt her back slide down the chair, until her weight rested mainly on her thighs and buttocks in the seat of the chair. Vladimir looked around with a wide-eyed expression, and she could see how quickly he was breathing. The green light above the control panel lit up once more.

Verity unfastened her seatbelt and stood, feeling uncomfortably heavy. She stretched and tried a few paces, her feet dragging. "You can get up now."

Vladimir got out of the chair. He looked at his feet. He staggered slightly. Verity knew what it was that was disconcerting him. The wall, or rather the floor, when the centrifuge was operational, was angled to compensate for Callisto's own gravity, and this meant the walls were not quite vertical in a way that created a subtle but uncanny optical illusion of being offbalance, and it took everyone a while to become accustomed to it.

Verity walked at a quick pace, in a circuit around what had previously been the walls. She passed Vladimir again, and went to one of the treadmills. "Oh, and if you use those weights, you need to put them back in the holder and put the chain back on when you've finished, so they can't fall out."

"Oh great! I can't connect to the ANT either!" Vladimir realised, fiddling with some small dumb-bells.

"The centrifuge is surrounded by a metal cage. The signal gets blocked out."

"What's the point in doing exercises?" Vladimir sat down

hard on the weightlifting bench. "It's a waste of time and you get sweaty and disgusting. Isn't it enough to stop my muscles from atrophying if I just come in here for an hour or so once a day, and walk about a bit and then read a research paper or something?"

"No, it isn't." Verity jumped off the treadmill with it still running, and went over to him. She put the barbell in position on the bench and screwed weights onto each end. She lay on the bench with her knees bent, and started her usual fifty reps.

Vladimir crouched on the floor to one side. He put one of the dumb-bells on the floor in front of him, and watched it roll from side to side with vibration of the machine. Verity rolled her eyes at him between reps.

"What is it you actually *do*," said Vladimir, picking up the dumb-bell and getting to his feet.

"I'm a sergeant in the Meritocracy's Sky Force, research division. I should have thought it was obvious."

"That doesn't answer my question. I'm asking you what a sergeant in the Meritocracy's Sky Force, research division, actually does, aside from pump iron and ride horses into people, and be obsessed with martial arts from the Far East and generally rude and disagreeable."

Verity shook her hair and glared at him. "Yesterday I killed a spy who was trying to escape the complex with information."

"Spy? What spy?" Vladimir picked up another barbell. He held it with both hands and straightened his arms above his head.

"I didn't speak to him. Probably he was Russian." Verity muttered under her breath, *thirty-seven*.

"How can anyone be a spy when there are only two exemptions from the Freedom of Information Act?" Vladimir sat down on the opposite bench, a dumb-bell in each hand.

"Well, clearly by stealing information that fits into one of the exemption categories." *Forty.* "All data has to be available to any member of the Electorate, which includes military and research information, but there are the two exemptions of data from original research that has not yet been published, and information that concerns individuals' private details. Considering this is a research base where humans live, it could have been either of those, or it could also have been that he was not a member of the Electorate and was in fact a foreigner from an enemy country." *Forty-five*.

"So which was it, then?"

Forty-six. "I dunno."

Vladimir dropped his hands, leaning his forearms on his thighs so the dumb-bells dangled. "You don't know? You killed someone for a reason you don't know?"

"It has to have been for one of those reasons, or there wouldn't have been an order to stop him gone through the ANT. I can find out what the reason was any time I like!"

"But you didn't?"

Verity reached fifty and levered the barbell back onto the stand. She sat up. "I can't now, because we're in the centrifuge. It wouldn't tell me the information he stole anyway, because that would be exempt from the Freedom of Information Act. All it would say was whether it was unpublished research, personal information, or foreign theft."

"And what, you don't know which of those it was? You don't care?"

"Well, no, I don't!" said Verity. "It's not important which it is. All that's important is that he stole information, and I stopped him from getting away with it!" She glanced at the readout on the control panel. "Our hour's almost up. I've wasted most of it talking to you. We had better put this gear back."

"Does Commodore Smith have you train all the newcomers

because of your scintillating people skills?" Vladimir said as he went back to the seats.

Verity reminded herself that she ought to try harder at this. Vladimir might be reporting back to Smith on how she conducted herself for all she knew. He wasn't exactly making it easy for her. Why did he have to be so dismissive and apathetic about the training and everything? If he'd been like Gecko, training him would be easy. She thought about what Vladimir had said as she took a chair and fastened her seatbelt. Although she said nothing to him, she made a mental note to look up the reason for the warrant later that day. Perhaps it would shed some light on the uneasy feeling she still had about John Aaron.

"I've booked one of the horse centrifuges for an hour commencing in twenty minutes," she said as they disembarked. "So if we come back and someone else is using it, there's going to be hell to pay."

They walked back down the main corridor and went to the horse block.

The stable where the horse Verity had ridden yesterday was kept, the one John Aaron had absconded with, stood empty, the racks opposite it unoccupied. The stable beside it that had housed the horse the spy had taken, the one that had fallen, was also empty, but the saddle and armour had been returned. Seeing an empty stable with tack laid out before it gave Verity an odd, lonely feeling. None of the horses had names; it was intended to stop people becoming attached to them, yet they all had their own personalities. Verity recalled the dead horse used to like being brushed, although it hated having its tail combed and its mane clipped. She supposed another horse would have to be shipped in now, and it would live in the dead horse's stable.

"Okay," Verity began in a low voice. "Rule one about fearless horses. Never stare a horse in the face. That's horse language for a threat. These horses are all fight and no flight, and if you stare at them you're going to get hurt."

She glanced over her shoulder to see Vladimir making notes on a writing slate with a stylus, and sighed. "Why are you writing it down?"

Vladimir raised his eyes to her nervously. "In case I forget."

"Most of it's just common sense."

He shrugged in a passive sort of way. Verity heard a tail swished, and breath blown loudly through a horse's nostrils. One of the animals towards the back of the stable crunched pellet food noisily, while two others groomed one another's necks over the partition dividing their loose boxes. She listened to the sounds of the animals before continuing, keeping her voice quiet. "Horses have their own social hierarchy, but it's not developed or maintained by aggression. These are bred to have such a temperament and reared in such a way that they readily accept humans as being their leaders, and as long as you listen to what they are telling you and give them consistent leadership, and don't do anything threatening towards them, they won't ever think to question that."

As she had been speaking, she had stood just outside the stallion's box, with her side facing the door, glancing occasionally in the direction of the horse but not looking straight at him. As she had expected, he reached his nose over the door, one ear forward and the other twitching side-to-front, and blew air through his nostrils at her. She reached up and rubbed his long, bony face

"See that big horse, in the stall where you first come in? She's the alpha mare. When you..." She broke off to stare at Vladimir's collapsed posture. "Actually, just don't look at her and keep out of her space. It's only me and Sergeant Black and the Commodore who are supposed to handle her anyway."

"Well, perhaps I should be handling her as well. It's going to be no good if I have to handle the stallion because no-one else wants to, and she comes into oestrus tomorrow and I have to cover her with him."

Verity shook her head. "Mares don't come into oestrus unless specific day length conditions are met. The lights in here are set up so they don't trigger that. It makes the horses more predictable and easier to handle."

Vladimir glanced at the horse, and then at Verity. "But the base's ANT has been operating the lights under a revised program, commencing just before the stallion's arrival here, that should bring them into oestrus soon."

"What? No-one told me."

Vladimir frowned. "No-one has to tell you. It's on the ANT. Anyone can access it. I thought research personnel were supposed to keep themselves up to date on matters concerning their research and the facility." Vladimir narrowed his eyes. "Unless you were too busy pumping lead and gallivanting about hunting *spies*."

Verity stared at him. How dare he speak to her like that! Well, she would show him in the centrifuge. She unlocked the stallion's stable door. "Let's sort this horse out, then."

When she reached up to sync her interface with him, she noticed that he was not completely black, like the other horses, but had a white star on his face, in the same position as his implant. She stroked his neck while she waited for him to adjust to interfacing with someone he'd not met before. Unlike the female horses, she picked up a prickling charge of randiness from him, and a feeling of constantly searching for something.

Stepping up to his left shoulder, his size overwhelmed her. He must have been more than nineteen hands, and the thick arch of his neck and glossy, well-muscled flanks made him so much more substantial than the mares. She gave him the thought-prompt to lift his foot, and he obeyed, and his hoof in her hand felt more like one of the weights that went on the barbell in the centrifuge than something belonging to a living animal. She checked the three implants in the middle of the foot. Unlike the other horses at the facility, whose longer hair was trimmed short to make it easier to care for, the stallion had feathered feet and a full-length mane.

"Before you shoe him, you need to use the file on his hoofs." She held out her hand. "Give it here. Now watch."

Vladimir observed as she clamped the leg between her knees and drew the steel rasp across one side of the hoof, then the other. "See, evenly like that. A farrier comes to do them properly every few months. Now you take over." She reached to her forehead and cut the connection.

Vladimir tuned his interface to the horse. Verity watched as he sidled alongside, patting the stallion's neck. He did the thought-prompt wrong, and the horse lifted his left foot. Stroking the animal's shoulder, he tried again, and this time got it right. She saw how carefully he cradled the hoof in both hands, as though he feared the tiniest crudity in his handling might harm this huge beast.

"Right, now put these shoes on him," she said, handing them to him. "They're for padding to stop him from hurting himself and damaging anything if he decides to have a panic in the centrifuge."

She watched him secure the shoes using the spanner. "I take it he's not been broken in?"

"No," Vladimir replied. "He's only been taught basic handling commands. He's a stud horse."

"Usually we ride the horses in the centrifuge in order to exercise them most effectively. He needs to be broken in."

"There shouldn't be a problem with it, in theory. I engineered him to be docile."

"I'll get him measured for tack. For now, we'll have to make do with just walking him. Put his headcollar on." Verity held it out. "No, not like that! It goes the other way round."

As Vladimir led the stallion out, his hand on the fastened

headcollar, the horse made a lunge for one of the mare's stalls, pulling Vladimir after him. "Don't let him do that!" Verity admonished him. "Know in your mind that he's not allowed to do stuff like that, and he'll feel it and he won't do it!"

"Okay." Vladimir's jaw was set in concentration as he got the stallion back under control. Out in the corridor the horse did a big hop in the unfamiliar gravity, and then reared up, pulling Vladimir off his feet.

"Please, can you take over, at least for a little while until he gets used to being out?" His face was white, beads of sweat standing out around a brow lined with nervousness. In one way Verity felt a perverse satisfaction in seeing him fail and back out. All theory and no practicality, this man. On the other hand, she was annoyed about having to stand over him and his horse like a nanny.

"All right, disconnect yourself and get out of the way."

Verity re-synced herself to the horse, preparing herself for the strange feelings he stirred in her. She forced herself into horse mentality as she led him onwards into the corridor. *I'm the alpha mare, and I know where I'm going. You follow me, because you don't know where you're going, and without me you'll be alone and scared with no friends. You're a stallion, and your job's to follow and protect us from other stallions and predators.*

"Don't walk behind him," she snapped at Vladimir. "Walk ahead of him, like he'd expect of someone worthy for him to follow!"

Vladimir skirted the horse to walk ahead, on the other side. But interfacing with the stallion made Verity feel strange, and she found herself staring at the shape of the man's bottom inside his shorts.

In the entrance to the centrifuge, the horse sniffed at the door. Verity waited patiently for him to examine it before stepping in through the entrance and giving him the encouragement to follow her. She'd never heard of a horse that could fear being centrifuged before. She had no idea what was about to happen, or whether she'd be able to control him.

"We need him to lie down, with his legs towards the wall." Verity indicated to Vladimir, and he put his hands against the horse's flank and turned his rump into position as Verity turned his head about. She gave the thought-prompt to lie. He put down his head, and his feet moved, but he remained standing. Verity closed her eyes and focused. She did not want Vladimir to see her lose control of an animal. She repeated the prompt, and this time the stallion dropped his head and gingerly put down on the knees of his forelegs. His hindquarters followed, and he settled on the floor with his legs tucked beneath him.

"Okay," she said in a low voice. "Just let him adjust. He's got to be calm when we secure him."

They both stroked the horse until he lay his neck down and relaxed onto his side. His eye remained turned towards them, the white showing. Verity fastened the thick securing belt around his girth. She used a foot thought-prompt to get him to give her his front hoof and let her extend his leg so it was straight and she could secure it in the strap. The second foot was attached to the same strap as the first on a short lead, and the same procedure was repeated on his hind feet.

Verity took the chair beside the horse's head. "You do the controls," she told Vladimir. "Close the door, and then start the centrifuge when you're ready and in your seat."

She watched him carry out the procedure, checking he did everything in the right order. When the motor started, she reached over to the stallion and scratched behind his ears, concentrating on transmitting calm thoughts to him. As the sliding sensation on her back began, he struggled, his fettered hoofs banging weakly against the grip on the floor and his neck pulling back. Verity closed her eyes again, forcing herself to centre on that feeling of calm. The wall slowly became the floor, and the stallion's hoofs touched down.

She undid her seatbelt. The horse was nervous about the uncanny walls. He stood with his head hanging, watching his feet.

"How did they take him on the ship?" she asked, patting the horse's neck.

"He had to be sedated," Vladimir explained. "They refused to have an animal like that on board otherwise."

"You sedated him? For a week or however long it took to get here from Torrmede? Don't you think that's inhumane? Wouldn't it be better for him if you just brought semen samples from him?"

"The project's not just about getting horses pregnant on Callisto. It's to make sure the horse as an animal is able to go through its ordinary breeding behaviour in it's entirety on Callisto. We need an actual stallion to prove that."

Verity glared at Vladimir, and stroked the stallion with newfound respect. "We can set him loose, now. I think he's settled down. You take over here."

"I'm not sure," he complained. "What if he panics?"

Verity touched her implant to sever her connection. She glared fiercely at Vladimir. "Then learn to make him not panic!"

Vladimir synced himself while she undid the securing straps. "We can't ride him so it's not safe to try to make him go fast. We'll just have to try and get him used to being walked round." She set off, walking, and Vladimir followed, leading the horse. They did one lap, so they were back at the seats, and then Verity glanced back and saw the stallion lifting up his tail. "Hey, watch what he's doing!"

Vladimir turned too late. A green-brown lump extruded itself from the horse and fell with a heavy thud to the floor. "Oh, great! Now we have to clean the centrifuge!"

Vladimir began to laugh.

"What could possibly be funny?" Verity frowned at him.

"I don't know," he said, still laughing. "In Soviet Russia, centrifuge cleans you!"

Feeling a sudden release of tension, Verity started to laugh as well. "In Meritocracy, horse shit on floor. In Soviet Russia, horse shit on *you!*"

Two laps later, Vladimir stepped in the manure and trampled footprints of it along the length of the floor, but Verity only laughed at this as well. The horse had stopped being nervous, and he hadn't kicked the centrifuge in, and it felt as though the ordeal was over and she had achieved something by centrifuging a horse that could fear.

They strapped the horse back to the wall and scraped the dung into a bag. Verity took control of him again as they turned off the motor, and together they led him out and back to the stables.

"You take his shoes off, so I can check you remembered how to do it," she told him.

"You're still interfaced to him."

"I'll tell him when to pick his feet up."

As Vladimir leaned over to tend to the horse's foot, his sweaty shirt rode up his back, revealing a gap of pale flesh between the hem and his belt. The stallion arched his neck to reach with his nose, and began to lick the skin, smacking his lips loudly. The man started and stifled a yelp when the horse's tongue touched him. "Are you making him do that?"

"No!"

"Why's he doing it, then?"

Verity shrugged. "Because you've been sweating, and there are salts on your skin and they taste nice to him."

He bent over again, suppressing laughter from the licking, and removed the shoe. Verity noticed again how gentle he was with the stallion's feet. He put the shoes on the rack outside, and took off the headcollar and hung it up.

"Thank you for helping me," he said politely, after closing the stable door. "I'm sorry to be such a pain in the arse, really."

"It's all right," she said. She gazed at him, taking in the dishevelled hair, smeary spectacles, and the way his sweaty shirt stuck to him. Those shorts really were ludicrous. She could practically taste the musky, sweaty smell of him in her own mouth, from when the stallion had licked him. "I'll see you tomorrow, same time?"

"Okay, then."

Verity went back to her quarters. She had a meeting in an hour's time, and she still had her normal daily horse exercising duty to do — it was her turn to work the alpha horse today.

In her quarters, she headed straight for the shower. It wasn't until the hot water was running over her that she remembered the conversation in the centrifuge. She quickly skimmed through the ANT's log of yesterday's events. There it was: *Spy, identity pending, apprehend/terminate. Nature of warrant: pending.*

Whoever had filed the record must have filled it in wrong. She'd have to report that to the Commodore. She tried to send a request to him, but the ANT couldn't locate him. He must be in the centrifuge, or outside the base beyond the ANT's main beacon's reach. He'd be going to the meeting, so perhaps if she went to his office she could catch him before that.

She hurriedly finished rinsing and turned the shower off. After she got dressed, she headed to the Commodore's office. There was no answer when she banged on the door. She heard hurried footsteps in the corridor, and went to see if that was him. It wasn't. Lloyd smiled as he passed, equipment and a suitcase under his arms. "Hi, Verity."

"Have you seen Commodore Smith?"

Lloyd raised his eyebrows. "Not today."

Another thought occurred to Verity. "Did you finish

getting information out of that head?"

"Oh, yes. Disposed of it, now. Didn't suffer."

"Did you find out anything about the information he'd stolen?"

"Yes, it'll be going in my report to the relevant authorities. Don't worry about it, you acted in accordance with the warrant."

"I'm not worrying about it. I was wondering more about the nature of the information he was trying to steal."

"Oh, well I obviously can't divulge that to you, because the information is to do with something that's exempt from the Freedom of Information Act."

"I know, but there seems to be an error in the ANT's log. It should say which exemption clause it satisfies, but it's just coming up with *pending*."

"Oh. Well, that's an error. I'll see if I can get round to fixing that later. It's exempt under the unpublished original research clause."

"Was there anything..." Verity stared at him. "Was there anything to do with me in the spy's mind? If there was, I'm entitled to know what it was under the act."

Lloyd looked her up and down. Could he see what she was thinking? Inquisitors were the only people able to mind interface directly to other people. Ordinary untrained people could detect the broadcasts others gave off when they felt strong emotions, and it was people who were particularly sensitive to these who were recommended for training as inquisitors. Perhaps Lloyd could sense Verity's fears and hopes that she thought she kept well enough screened off from other people. He took a step closer to her. "No, there was nothing about you." He continued in a low voice, "Something's troubling you. Why do you think you'd be involved in the information?"

"Because John Aaron attacked me, and he's still missing. I think it might have something to do with the spy."

Lloyd narrowed his eyes, tilting his head to one side. "I've always known there was something about you... Something both pride and shame, yet at the same time, you fear others learning of it."

Verity stood, eyes locked with his, and neither spoke for a moment.

Lloyd said, "I have to leave for the orbital in two days, and I have a lot of things to sort out, but I can spare a few moments to speak to you, if you feel you have something you'd like to get off your mind."

In the Inquisitor's lab, Verity was relieved to see the bench where the head had stood had been cleared away. She took a seat by Lloyd's desk while he made some tea.

"Can I speak in confidence?" she said as he placed down a mug for her.

"Certainly." Lloyd gestured outwards with his hands, palms up. "Keeping the Meritocracy's secrets is my business. Anything you say to me won't leave this room."

Verity paused, composing what she was going to say. "Private Aaron tried to kill me, because he was an extremist belonging to some sort of cult."

Lloyd took a sip of tea, and nodded.

"He knew something else about me, something that to him made me blasphemous to his beliefs by the very act of my birth. Do you know about Pilgrennon's experiments?"

"Of course. Who doesn't?"

"Pilgrennon's research is respected these days, but when he did it over 100 years ago it was illegal. In the earlier days of the Meritocracy, genetic modification of humans was only allowed to eliminate genetic disease. It was barely twenty years ago there was a second referendum on it, that the Electorate voted to lift the ban, and allow genetic modification on humans, provided all genetic material used came from humans."

"Of course."

"That referendum was passed a year before I was born."

Lloyd raised his eyebrows. "Ah."

Verity inhaled deeply. "The company that created me were licensed to continue work with the genetics Pilgrennon had created." She paused. "Did you know any of this already?"

"No."

"I thought you might have been able to... tell what I was thinking."

Raising his eyebrows and smiling slightly, Lloyd interlocked his fingers together on the desk before him. "I can invade people's conscious thoughts." He lowered his chin, raising his eyes to her. "But if I tried it on you, you'd know it."

Verity considered this. It made sense. "The things John Aaron said to me sounded like he'd found out I'm the offspring of Caleb."

A crease became visible on Lloyd's forehead, beneath the shunts and interface apparatus. "If that's a published experiment, there will be information on the ANTs. Any data that might identify you would be protected, but it would be possible for someone intent on digging deep to use the data to narrow down their search and potentially identify you."

"But I think there's more to it than that. I've just got this *feeling* about it. What if the spy was involved with that as well? What if there are several of them, and they've got a camp set up on Callisto, somewhere out of range of the ANT, and that's where Private Aaron has gone?"

Suddenly Lloyd let off a snort that petered out to a snigger. "I mean no insult, Verity, but surely you can't fail to appreciate the irony. If you were engineered using Caleb's gametes, you're genetically Jananin Blake's grandchild, and for a descendant of someone who is widely credited as being one of history's greatest rational thinkers to say there's a problem because she has an intuitive feeling... *well!*"

"I don't mean like that! I mean, a feeling like when you do a calculation and the result's the wrong magnitude, or when there's an equation with the constant missing!"

Lloyd was shaking his head, still chuckling. "I'm sure it's nothing. There wasn't anything to indicate anything of that nature in the spy's mind." His face became serious, his head-shaking more emphatic.

"There's something. There has to be something I've missed."

Lloyd downed the rest of his tea. "Ah, well. *Ignotum per ignotius*. I'm sorry, Verity, but I really must get on with my packing now. I'm sorry this is troubling you. I hope it all starts to make sense soon, and that talking to me has helped consolidate some things for you." He pushed back his chair.

"Thanks," said Verity, standing up. *Not really*, she thought. Or maybe it had. Something was missing from this puzzle, and now she'd had an idea about where she might start looking for it.

chapter four

NEXT MORNING, after supervising Vladimir and the stallion in the centrifuge, Verity watched him unshoe the horse and lock up the stable.

"Pick a horse," she said, spreading her arms, palms up.

Vladimir stared at her. "What? What for?"

"I'm going to teach you to ride."

Vladimir's eyes widened and his brows went up.

"For that stallion to get the exercise he needs, he needs to be ridden in the centrifuge, and for that to happen, you need to learn to ride, and he needs to learn to be ridden. If you both try to learn at once, you'll only teach each other mistakes. So pick a horse; any horse other than the stallion or the big mare."

Vladimir turned 360 degrees, examining the horses. "Are there any that are... *nice*?"

"They're all nice. They're animals. Animals don't do pettiness and jealousy, and grudges and nastiness."

"All right, that one." Vladimir singled out a horse with its head over the stable door, watching him.

"Put her outdoor tack and shoes on. When you've finished, I'll inspect how you've done it."

As Vladimir approached the horse cautiously and reached to its face to tune his interface, Verity went to the alpha mare. If she was teaching him to ride, the lead horse's presence would reinforce that. She touched the horse's implant to sync herself, and opened the stable door. Verity liked this horse, liked how she anticipated instructions and thought ahead, and how when she was with this horse, other riders and their horses fell into order as if by nature.

After she'd put the gear on, she went to inspect Vladimir's effort. The shoes and the basic tack were correct, but the stirrups and some of the fastenings on the armour were wrong.

"There's no bit on this bridle," Vladimir said.

"It's not good for them to have saliva running out of their mouths in the sort of temperatures outside. We use thought-prompts and a bridle with no bit to control them." After correcting the faults, Verity said. "I'm going to tell you something, but you're not allowed to say anything about it."

Vladimir tilted his head fancifully. "Isn't that in violation of the Freedom of Information Act?"

"No. Shut up and listen. I'm going to teach you to ride, and while we're out, we're going to take some measurements, so we have to take the bore kit. We're also going to take the climbing gear because I want to do something else. When I killed that spy the other day, I cut off his head and took it back to the Inquisitor as fast as I could, because he needed to find out what the spy knew. I left the rest of the spy's body behind, and it fell down a crater at the edge of the scarp so it won't have been recovered. Now I'm wondering if there was something the Inquisitor missed, and because he's disposed of the head now, I can't ask for him to look again, so I'm going to try to see if there are any other clues on the spy's body."

Vladimir widened his eyes and let out his breath in an exasperated huff. "How could the Inquisitor have missed it? They're trained to extract information from people's minds."

"He could have missed it, if it was something completely different to the data the spy had stolen. He wouldn't have known to look for it."

"If this data's exempt from the Freedom of Information Act, and you go looking for it and you find it, doesn't that mean you're committing a crime and you're essentially a spy?"

"I'm a member of staff here. It's not if there is any and I tell the Commodore I found it!"

"Why don't you tell the Commodore now, then? Before

you go looking for it?"

"Because it might be nothing. It's not based on anything concrete." In truth, Verity had felt an odd suspicion towards Commodore Smith ever since she'd admitted her concerns to him and he'd dismissed the idea that John Aaron might have been in league with the spy or someone else in the base.

"It sounds like a conspiracy theory." Vladimir's voice took on a sardonic tone. "You just don't want to lose face."

"No." Verity looked him fiercely in the eyes, as she might have done were she trying to intimidate an animal. "And you wouldn't, if you were in the same position. If you have a hypothesis for a scientific idea, do you go and tell your superiors before you've done any preliminary tests?"

"Well, that depends..."

"There, see? Now put these on." Verity opened the store cupboard and kicked some spare armour she'd got together that morning in his direction. She gathered up the climbing gear and half of the rods from the boring kit and began to load them into the bags behind her horse's saddle.

"This is too big," said Vladimir.

When Verity glanced back to him, he was struggling to fasten the chestpiece. "It's not too big; it's you that's too small. It's supposed to be adjustable anyway."

"Yes, well, I think I'm beyond the remit of its adjustability."

"Oh, come here!" Verity exhaled forcefully and rolled her eyes. "Put your arms up." She adjusted the straps at the sides of the armour, and snapped the buckles at the front shut. "There you are. You're not *that* weedy. Now put the rest of it on, and put this kit in your bag."

The sun had just cleared the horizon as they led the horses out. Jupiter, above the equatorial horizon as it always appeared from the latitude of the base, was waning close to its last quarter against an indigo sky. Morning sun glittered on the rime coating the concrete walls of the base. Verity looked up the side of the building, squinting in the glare. Another near semicircle, stark and greyish, hung just above Jupiter; probably Ganymede. The horses blew clouds of steam.

Verity jumped up, grabbing the front and back of the saddle, straightened her arms, and swung her knee over. She got her feet into the stirrups, wriggling her knees into position so her legs against the contours of the saddle pressed her firmly down into the seat. Vladimir put his foot on one of the building's buttresses to aid his mounting, and landed heavily on his horse.

When he was settled as best as he apparently could manage, Verity pointed to her saddle. "Make sure your knees are pressed in below the front edge of the saddle. The way it's shaped is designed to make it hard for you to be thrown upwards when you're sitting properly."

Vladimir squirmed, pushing his knees down and in so his heels went out awkwardly against the stirrups. "Is that right?"

"You look like you've got constipation," said Verity. "I suppose it'll have to do. We're going to go about a hundred yards and then stop to take a sample. Think you can manage that?"

Behind his visor, Vladimir grimaced. "I can try."

"Okay, then. Look, don't worry about the reins and the stirrups at the moment. Just stay focused and use thought-prompts properly. The horse knows to follow me, and it'll be able to sense what you want it to do from the interface."

"Focus," said Vladimir. "Easier said than done."

Verity touched her heels to the horse's flanks and gave the thought-prompt to move off, and they were away, out through the compound's gates and out onto the black ice plain that gleamed like obsidian in the morning sun. Hoofs clapping on the ice, snorts of breath rushing from the horse's nostrils over her shoulders and Verity's knees, the swaying motion of the gallop, the undulating ground opening out before her at exhilarating speed, Verity felt the horse's heartbeat as if it was her own, as though the beast and she were one.

About here would be right. She leaned back, tightening the reins and giving the command to slow. When the horse had come to a halt, she looked back and saw Vladimir following some distance away, at an uncontrolled and wobbly canter.

"There's no point trying to go medium speed in this gravity!" she shouted as he closed the distance. "Trotting and cantering has too much up-and-down movement! If you just gallop flat out it's smoother!"

Vladimir's horse slowed to a jolting trot before stopping beside Verity's. He looked uncomfortable and unnatural in the saddle, leaning too far forward and with his legs bent at the wrong angle. Verity kicked her feet out of the stirrups and slid off. She pulled the bore kit from the bag and began connecting the rods together.

Vladimir slid off his horse, landed off balance on his heels, and grabbed hold of his horse to steady himself, wisps of vapour escaping the dehumidifier-warmer on the mouthpiece of his helmet.

"What's this for again?"

Verity set the drill point on the ice and fastened the handle onto the rod. "It's for monitoring the temperature and composition of the ice. The idea with this moon is that the Meritocracy eventually wants it for a permanent colony. Callisto's not like Earth and Mars. It's made of ice and dust, and if it heats up too much it'll melt and turn into a ball of slush. One of the base's functions here is to monitor the temperature and make sure it remains stable."

"So what happens if it isn't?"

"If it gets above -20, that's not good. There'll be a report on it to go back to MANTIcore, and then probably the Electorate will nominate it for referendum, and then it'll have to be decided."

Vladimir set his arms akimbo and turned his head to survey the landscape. "It's not my field, but I'd imagine heating it up to a habitable temperature but not going so far that the ice melts must be a pretty delicate balance."

"It is." Verity leaned on the handle with both hands, pressing down on the drill. She turned the handle and felt the diamond teeth bite into the ice. "When they terraformed Callisto, they extracted carbon, nitrogen, and ice from the crust, split the ice into oxygen and hydrogen, and burned the carbon in the oxygen to produce a $N_2/O_2/CO_2$ atmosphere to kick-start global warming."

Vladimir looked vacant for a moment. Verity fancied she could see gears turning in his head. "What about the hydrogen?"

"That's what's used to power the fusion engine that generates power for the compound." Verity turned the handle again. "Here, you have a go at this."

Vladimir grasped the handle and twisted it. The point slid out of its indentation and scratched a white scar across the dark ice. Verity rolled her eyes.

"This thing's rubbish!" he argued. "Why don't you have a machine for doing this?"

"There's a motor in it. You need to start it off by hand. You hold the bottom of it and I'll do it."

Vladimir knelt on the ice and held the rod with both hands. Verity leaned on it, turning the handle again. After a few turns it was in deep enough to start the motor. They held the bore mount still and watched as the depth gauge on the readout in the centre of the handle rose.

The motor stopped, and a few seconds later a figure flashed on the dial, and the handle beeped.

"Do you need to write that down on a computer or something?" Vladimir asked.

"No need. I just record it real-time, into a spreadsheet on the ANT." Verity had already sent the recording back to the base with a thought-prompt. She pressed the button to retract the drilling shaft, and pulled the bore up from the ice. "Let's move on to the next one."

They took five more readings in this way, *en route* towards the scarp where Verity and John Aaron had chased the spy. As she came into the shadow of the great ice protrusions, Verity looked back to see Vladimir still lagging behind. "Hurry up!" she shouted. "Don't be such a wimp!"

After he caught up, he asked, "Is there any reason for this?"

"I just told you what the reason was!"

"I mean, why use horses? Why not use a vehicle? It's warm inside it, and you can't fall off."

Verity frowned. "Because most of the terrain's no good for vehicles. It's all right over there and around the base, but most of it's all ravines and mess." She pointed up the near vertical cliff. "Last time I came here, I went that way." She paused to relish the daunted expression he made. "But this time, we'll go the slow way. Now keep up with me!"

She kept to a slow canter as they followed the narrow path edged with sharp protrusions of ice and jagged outcrops. It wasn't really safe to go flat out with this little margin of error anyway, and she'd be held accountable if Vladimir managed to skewer himself on the ice, or even worse, if he hurt the horse through his ineptitude.

Verity could see through the horse's vision that Vladimir was twisting and shifting in his saddle to get a good view of the surroundings. "This really is quite spectacular! It's got to be in the same league as the Mariner Valley, or the Grand Canyon!"

"Whatever."

"But look at it! It's amazing! People would pay good money to come and look at this and have photographs of it." He added, in a more pensive voice, "I hope it doesn't melt into a ball of slush. Does it have a name?"

Verity had slowed her horse to a walk. "We just call it the scarp. They run all around the Valhalla crater. This happens to be the closest one to the installation. These towers and pointy bits of lighter ice are unusual, though. They come from when there's an impact and molten stuff from the mantle gets forced up through the crust and crystallises fast."

"I suppose before the moon was terraformed, they just used to sublime away, into those blunt columns you see on the plain?"

"Yes, that ice is older."

"We ought to think of a name for it!"

Verity threw a glance over her shoulder. "They can call it Sergeant Verity's Canyon."

"Like they're going to call it after you..."

"Well, they're not going to call it after you!"

"You never know. I could become a famous geneticist. Like Pilgrennon."

Verity's horse snorted. "What do you know about Pilgrennon? He wasn't Russian, and he did genetic engineering on humans, not horses."

Vladimir was staring up at the glittering crags. Verity followed his focus to the sharp cliff edge. "You know what else this reminds me of?" he said. "Torrmede."

Verity made a face. "How can it look like Torrmede? Stop name-dropping Torrmede into everything! Just because you went there doesn't make you special or anything like that."

"You know what I mean! Torrmede's built on a steep rocky piece of land, and the rhododendrons all grow up it."

"I never saw any rhododendrons at Torrmede or anywhere else that looked like ice spikes!" Verity checked the surrounding landmarks. This looked like the right place. On the ground she saw a lighter stripe scratched; could that mark where a horse had slipped? She dismounted.

"Now where are you going?" she heard Vladimir say. There was that smashed stand of ice she'd kicked over to pack the head in. There, the broken points where the horse had gone down. A queasy sensation started in Verity's stomach at the memory of the horse's death, and began to spread upwards into her chest. The base had recovered the horse's body, but a dark patch on the ice, frozen blood, showed where it had died. Here was where John Aaron had attacked her, and she had spared him. With a sudden apprehension, she raised her eyes to the empty hollows and jagged shadows of the scarp, sensing something unfamiliar and sinister about them. What if he had a way to survive out here, and he still lived, and still hunted her? What if malign eyes were upon her, right now?

She looked the other way, to the edge of the crater. That was where the spy's body had fallen. Crystals sprouted like crenellations from the edge of the path; she could see no sign of a descent, as she'd suspected. It wouldn't be worth ordering a party to climb into that crater and drag out a corpse when all the information the Inquisitor needed had been in the spy's mind.

"This is where I killed the spy," she told Vladimir as she pulled the mountaineering gear out of the bag. "Do you know how to abseil?"

"No. And if that's an offer, I don't want to either. I think learning to ride is enough for one day."

Verity picked up the chisel and hammer, and pressed the heating switch on the chisel. "It's probably best if you stay up here anyway for safety reasons."

Vladimir got down from his horse. "Good."

When the metal rod of the chisel glowed red, Verity pounded it into the ice with the mallet, with the tip pointed downwards towards the drop. The ice hissed as the chisel went in. She pulled it out and banged one of the pins into the hole, the melted ice sealing it there as it refroze. She repeated this at another point two feet away and parallel to the first pin. She donned a climbing harness and secured the rope to the pins.

With the rope connected to her belt, Verity pulled against the pins, testing them. She stepped to the edge of the path and kicked down, stamping off the ice stalagmites to clear a gap through which to descend. The fragments of ice rolled away down the side of the crater, dwindling away until they became imperceptible over distance.

Vladimir watched her, fiddling with his armour. "What am I supposed to do if you don't come back?"

"Well, go back to the base, of course. And I am going to come back!"

"Look, just supposing you die, what am I supposed to tell the Commodore you were doing?"

Verity shrugged. "Tell him the truth. I'm hardly going to care if I'm dead, am I? I'll be half an hour at most. Keep the horses in the sun, and walk them around a bit. It's only -25 so they should be okay."

"I thought you said I'm not supposed to touch the big horse?"

"Well, all right, you are allowed to touch her in these particular circumstances. But remember what I told you about them! I don't want to think up an excuse to tell the Commodore if I come back up here and she's trampled on you."

Verity took hold of the rope, gave it one more tug, and dropped backward off the path and began to abseil down into the crater. She soon fell into the rhythm of pushing off with her knees, letting the rope run, and bending her knees and taking up the slack in the rope as her feet came back against the wall. She noticed pock-marks, tiny craters, and irregularities in the surface — she'd need them on her way back up.

The gradient slowly began to decrease, and abseiling became harder. When the ground became level enough, she disconnected herself from the rope and turned to look around. The far side of the crag lay in an inky pool of shadow, the sun cradled in a rocky cusp on the rim. A few feet ahead, one of the fragments of ice she'd broken off at the edge of the path lay in a crater. He couldn't have landed far from here. She could make out an irregular lump in the crater basin, some distance away. She could still sense the horse's signal, although it was indistinct from distance. Through the big mare's vision, she could see Vladimir sitting on the ice near the pins.

She looked up at the rope snaking down from the path above. The crater was huge and looked pretty much the same from wherever you stood. What if she went down there looking for the corpse and couldn't find the rope again? That wouldn't do. Not seeing any other way to mark it, she pulled off her helmet and switched on the lamp on it, and set it down at the bottom of the rope. Cold air stabbed into the membranes of her nostrils and lungs, and her breath blossomed into white vapour when she exhaled. She felt vulnerable without her helmet, knowing that John Aaron might still be at large. Her eyes followed the rope up until distance swallowed it, to where she knew, but could not see, the path lay. Aaron might kill Vladimir, and follow her down the rope. Or he might disconnect the rope and throw it over, stranding her out here. Tense fear and doubt knotted about her innards. Perhaps it had not been a good idea to come here, looking for information she had no right to.

Well, she was here now, so she might as well get on with it. The sooner she found that body, the sooner she could leave.

She shuffled forward down the steep incline. As she drew closer, she saw the irregular object was indeed the spy's body, lying on its back with the arm still bent over the midriff towards the hip. Looking down on it, she could tell from the unnatural angle of the pelvis that the fall had broken the spine. Needles of ice had crystallised from the neck wound, giving the bloody flesh a fibrous, grainy appearance.

Verity crouched down to examine the corpse. He had worn no proper armour, just a standard type of ship-suit made from a closely woven insulating polymer fibre, with a lightweight armour waistcoat, boots, and gloves over it, all made up of durable fabric covered with plates of thin polymer alloy. A scarf unravelled from the head; he'd probably been trying to breathe through that, keeping his nose warm. He must have been desperate, and *freezing*, clinging to the back of that horse as he tried to flee from her and Aaron.

She frowned as she saw where his hand reached over to his hip. She could see no gun there, as she'd expected. Perhaps it had detached from him in the fall. From the way his fingers were poised, it looked as though he'd been reaching for a pocket on his waistcoat, beneath the belt. Verity grasped the arm, trying to move it out the way, but it was frozen solid. The hand felt like it was made of stone inside the glove. She rolled over the stiff body to get a better view of the pocket. The fabric of the waistcoat was still flexible, and she reached inside it. Through her glove, she could only feel a numb friction. Her fingers slid over something. She felt again, her hand closing over a small flat rectangle. She couldn't feel anything else in there.

She withdrew the glove. The object was just a white card, with a name, and a hologram and familiar coat of arms — a Torrmede alumnus's card. She had one herself, very similar to that. There was no weapon.

She'd killed an unarmed man.

She bent her head over the card, trying to read the characters embossed on the surface in the weak sunlight. *Anthony Cornelian, MSc*. She glanced at the body again, its arm frozen with the hand over the pocket. There was nothing else he could have been reaching for apart from this card. So why would he possibly think a Torrmede alumnus's card would be of any use to him, against someone armed with a katana?

With fingers made clumsy by her gloves, she turned the card over. On its back was a geometric rendition of a flowering tree, with a similarly stylised owl perched in the fork of the trunk. The sigil of the Magnolia Order. She had killed an unarmed man, and a fellow of the Order?

Now she'd rolled over the corpse, she noticed a bulkiness about the back in its new position. A backpack. She crawled forward and undid the clasp on it. The top flap was all stained with frozen blood that cracked and fell away in dry flakes when she eased it back. The edge of a thin, flat object showed inside its recesses. Verity pulled it out. A computer slate. There wasn't anything else in the main compartment of the bag, and the only thing she could find in the pockets was what looked like a plastic key with a circuit embedded in it. Leaving the computer and the card lying on the ice, she rolled the body back into its former position, and checked the other waistcoat pocket, stuck down against a thigh that felt like a frozen ham wrapped in a cloth. Nothing.

Gathering up the computer and the card and device, she got to her feet, looking down at the corpse once more. It felt different to be looking at the headless body and knowing it had belonged to someone of the Magnolia Order. Suddenly the dead spy had become a person, not stolen data. With a shudder, she turned away and walked briskly back to the place where the light of her helmet showed. She'd not thought to bring a bag, so she had to improvise one by wrapping her cloak around the computer and stuffing the hem of it through her belt. Her ears, her nose, and even her eyeballs felt frozen as she put the helmet back on.

Climbing back up got the blood flowing again and warmed her. Her shoulders were aching by the time she got to the top and reached up to pull herself over.

"Oh there you are, finally!" said Vladimir, grabbing her by the elbow and helping pull her up. "Did you find your data?"

"Maybe." Verity pulled the computer out of her cloak and

stowed it in the bag on her horse.

"You probably won't get anything from that," said Vladimir, noticing the computer. "I expect it got smashed up in the fall, and then it's been frozen."

"We'll see." Verity mounted her horse. "Pull those pins out and let's get back to the base."

Back at the base, Verity told Vladimir to wait outside with the horses while she went in and fetched a roll of plastic film. She wrapped it around the cold computer to stop water from condensing on it and damaging it when it was brought back into the warm air. She saw to her horse quickly, took the computer back to her billet and dumped it on her bed, and then went back to the stables to make sure Vladimir had seen to his horse properly. He said he had to read a research paper, and went off after that, and she was glad to have some time to herself to look into things.

Back in her quarters, the plastic wrapping on the computer was covered with beads of dew, and a damp patch was beginning to spread across the bedcover. She wiped the moisture off the computer, but it was still painfully cold to touch.

She took out the card again, and examined it. Anthony Cornelian. She ran a search on the name through the ANT, and it came back with no matches. There weren't and never had been any personnel registered to the base with that name. She went back to the records for the morning the arrest warrant had been issued on the spy. She noticed the entry had been changed, to *Freedom of Information violation, unpublished research theft*. Scanning through the records of the day, she couldn't find anything else relating to it. She gave the command to the ANT to compile a list and any fragments of any files or data that had been deleted between two hours before and four hours after the arrest warrant had been issued.

She went back to the computer. It still felt cold to touch, but the moisture on the surface was much lesser now. She peeled off the plastic, wiping the computer off on her uniform. Carefully, she pressed the on key mounted on the side of the unit.

The screen lit up — the computer still worked! Verity found its signal. *Damn.* It was protected by an owner imprint. Verity used the same software with her own computers; a simulation of her own personality and consciousness as imparted through the interface to create an individually customised firewall. After all, who knows better than you what files you don't want to be viewed by your mother, or your boss, or some stranger you've never met?

She stared at the computer. There was no way of removing an imprint, short of wiping the drive and destroying all the data. It was unlikely she'd be able to get it to reveal anything to her, but it would cost nothing to try, she supposed.

She pressed the sync button on the side of the unit, and reached to her forehead to tune her interface to it.

Unrecognised operator. Access denied.

Lying to a computer was a pointless endeavour. Verity got straight to the point. *Anthony Cornelian is dead, killed for failure to comply with an arrest warrant from the Meritocracy on grounds of spying and violation of an exemption to the Freedom of Information Act. I have reason to suspect his death may have been a miscarriage of justice and his arrest warrant a forgery. I cannot substantiate my suspicions without further information, data which I have reason to believe may be stored in this unit. Will you permit me access to such data?*

For what felt like a long time, the computer did not respond.

Eventually a reply came back. *Are you Zeta Verity?*

Verity started back from the computer. *How do you know who I am?*

If you are Zeta Verity, then Anthony Cornelian is indeed dead, and I have no doubt it was you who killed him.

chapter five

IN THE REFECTORY, Verity stacked her rations of fibre loaf and levigated esculents onto a tray. *If you know stuff about me*, she thought to the computer in her pocket, *I'm entitled to know it under the Freedom of Information Act.*

The Freedom of Information Act applies to humans and ANTs. I don't fit in to either of those categories. The voice in Verity's head was a rich male tenor, with a Martian accent and a slightly haughty parlance.

What category do you fit into, then? Verity demanded as she scanned the refectory for an empty table, and found one near the windows.

I'm a closed security system. I'm not going to divulge the information I have to you or anyone or anything else. Data storage protection is exempt from the Act in order that it can be programmed to be impenetrable so old computers can be disposed of without risk of leakage.

Yes, but you're not an ordinary security system. You're an imprint of a person, and people are not impenetrable, they're fallible! Verity covered the distance to the table in long angry strides.

Well, perhaps I am fallible. I'm not sure yet. I've not decided whether you're a friend or an enemy of Anthony Cornelian.

I've already told you, I'm neither. I killed you, but I was obeying an order and I had a warrant for your arrest, and I told you to stop, and you didn't, and you reached for some stupid Torrmede card, and I thought it was a weapon so I killed you. Verity slammed her tray down on the table and dragged a chair across the floor. *Why do you even care? You're an imprint; you're not actually him. You only even exist when someone tries to use this computer. He's dead and you're just a ghost in a machine.*

Something almost like a laugh forced itself into Verity's

imagination. *I don't feel like a ghost. Not since you started playing around with me.*

Verity stopped halfway through ripping open a cardboard carton. *Right. I'm switching you off.*

Fine. Turn me off. I know you'll only turn me right back on again.

Urh! Verity made a face as she arranged her food on the table. *You're annoying! I'd want to kill you, if I hadn't already done it!*

She stuffed the food into her mouth, chewing for as little time as possible before swallowing.

This food is awful! said the voice in her head. *What are you, a vegetarian or something?*

Verity almost choked. *You can taste what I'm eating?*

Sure thing. I can see it too, and it doesn't look any better.

Verity rolled her eyes. Bleedback.

She's nice, the ghost of Anthony Cornelian remarked as Verity caught sight of a woman, a little older than herself, putting food on a tray. *Look down a bit.*

That's Sergeant Black, thought Verity disgustedly, *and she wouldn't be very pleased if she thought I was ogling her tits.* She looked away from Sergeant Black to see Vladimir with a tray, smiling ingratiatingly and walking towards her.

He's nice too.

No he isn't.

Why not? Nerds can be sexy.

Vladimir set down his tray, and a computer similar to the one in Verity's pocket. "I'm so hungry, even this horrible food looks enticing. So, did that computer work?"

"Oh, it works." Verity glared at him. "Only there's nothing useful on it apart from an arsy bisexual ghost." In the back of her mind, Anthony Cornelian made a tut-tutting noise.

Vladimir raised one eyebrow and twisted his mouth. He ripped open his carton, spilling the contents on the table and his own computer. "Damn!"

Verity watched him wipe up the mess before continuing. "Want to see something else I found?" She set down the spy's Torrmede card, on the opposite side of the table to Vladimir's food. She put her own card next to it.

After studying them for a moment, Vladimir fumbled in his pocket and brought out another Torrmede card, and put it with the other two. "Snap. So what? Like you said to me not so long ago, an association with Torrmede doesn't make you special."

Verity reached across and turned over her and Anthony Cornelian's cards, showing the matching images on the backs.

Lines formed on Vladimir's forehead. "What's that?"

Verity sighed. "It's a Magnolia Order insignia."

"Ah." Vladimir picked up his card and turned it so the unadorned back faced towards Verity. "Is that what makes you special, then? What exactly is the Magnolia Order?"

"It's a society. Jananin Blake and Takahashi Yūtarō founded it."

"And you belong to it? This is something to do with those martial arts swords you've got, isn't it?"

"It's called iaido. Technically it means something like 'the way of being mentally alert and ready to react' but in practice it's about swords."

"So, this Magnolia Order. Is it a division of the Meritocracy's military?"

"No, it's autonomous from the Meritocracy."

"What, so you have votes among its members about what you're going to do, and whether you're going to send spies to research bases on ice moons?"

"No."

"Well, that doesn't sound very meritocratic." Vladimir raised his eyebrows in a sardonic sort of way.

Verity glowered at him. "It is meritocratic. People without merit aren't allowed to join it."

"Who's in charge of it, then?"

"I don't know. Probably the people who have been in it longest."

Vladimir snorted. "Sounds dodgy."

"Who are you to say what sounds dodgy? You're a Not-a-Proper-Doctor from a country where people don't have full meritocratic rights!"

Vladimir scraped out the carton and licked his spoon. "All I'm saying is it sounds Masonic, and like exactly the sort of organisation that would send spies to places to steal research data that's exempt from the Freedom of Information Act."

"There's more to it than that," said Verity quietly.

"What more?"

"The spy knew what my name was."

Vladimir shrugged. "He probably looked you up on the ANT."

"No, he knew who I was the instant I tried to access the computer. My name's mixed up with this somehow. Either the spy was an infiltrator and he was in league with John Aaron and they were both trying to kill me, or the spy was here for some other purpose to do with John Aaron and whoever else he's in league with that's being covered up, and John Aaron set out to kill both me and him."

Vladimir looked at her as if she was mad. "Well, whatever they were up to, if they're both dead, they can't be up to it any more."

"We don't know that John Aaron is dead," said Verity. "He absconded."

"If he went outside, he must be dead by now."

"What if there's a camp somewhere that's been set up by some subversive organisation, or spies from a non-meritocratic country? There's no satellite surveillance here and no GPS, so it could happen."

"Hmm," said Vladimir. "Well, I don't know. I need to go and work on my thesis now." He pushed back his chair, picked up his computer, and headed off through the main doors.

Verity drained her glass and stood up from the table. The picture of Worrall had been taken off the wall, replaced with an illustration of a gleaming city spread out over an icy landscape beneath a full midnight Jupiter, presumably someone's vision of what Callisto might look like once it was fully settled. Verity wasn't in the mood to write on the wall. She went back to her quarters.

What do you know about John Aaron? she asked, dumping the computer on the bed.

Nothing. I've never heard the name before.

That or you just won't tell me.

If I couldn't tell you, I'd say so.

Verity checked her inbox. The ANT had finished collecting all the file fragments she'd requested, and had them ready for her to read. Verity felt restless and mentally dishevelled, and she didn't feel at all like sitting down and reading through them all now. She'd take a horse for a run in the centrifuge, she decided. That should clear her head. Perhaps things would start to add up after that.

As she reached over to switch the computer off, it said to her, *I will point one thing out to you. The data on this computer is off-limits, but anyone can read from it when the owner last logged on.*

Verity found the date. "That was the day before the arrest warrant was issued," she murmured. "So he must have found whatever data he was looking for in the time between, and he never interfaced to the computer knowing it, so you're saying you don't know it?"

Correct.

She headed wearily for the horse block.

A bad atmosphere that Verity couldn't pin down permeated the stables. When she went to a horse and synced to it, there was something ugly in its temperament. *Oh, be calm*, she thought, putting her hand to its neck to soothe it as it threw its head up, rolling its eyes and flicking its tail. She sent the thought-prompt to the horse's monitoring system for a status report on its condition. When the report came back, there was something out of order — something she'd never seen on the feedbacks of any of the horses here. It took a few seconds for her to work it out. The horse had come into oestrus.

Damn. Verity closed the stable door. Vladimir, where was Vladimir? The ANT said he was in his quarters, but when she tried to message him there was a DND warning on his interface. *Idiot*. This was his project, and this was the inevitable outcome of it, and he should have been alert to it. As Verity was calculating from the ANT's information where Vladimir's quarters were and what was the best route, the stallion put his head over his stable door, broadcasting lust and frustration. His neck strained towards the ovulating mare's stall, and he pulled his upper lip back over his teeth and sucked in a draught of air.

"Yes, all right!" said Verity to him angrily. "You can have your evil way with her when I find Vladimir!" She ran back into the main corridor and made her way to the lower floor and the room the ANT told her Vladimir lived in. She pounded the door with her fist. "Vladimir!"

The door opened after a moment. "Verity, I'm trying

to work." Vladimir's hair was dishevelled, his glasses were propped up on his forehead, and the top three buttons of his shirt were unfastened.

Verity found herself staring at the gap in his shirt, annoyance and disapproval mingling with something else. "You look more like you've been asleep! And this is your work; a mare's in oestrus!"

"Damn! I'm sorry." Vladimir hurried into the corridor, doing up his shirt as he went. "You should have told me."

"I did tell you! If you hadn't told the ANT you were DND, you would have heard!"

"Sorry," said Vladimir again.

Verity turned to face to him, taking hopping quicksteps backward as she spoke. "Stop saying sorry, just don't do it again!"

The stallion whinnied as they came through the stable block door. Vladimir's eyes became wide. "Wait here," Verity told him. "I'll take the mare out to the corral first, and then we'll come back for him."

Verity re-synced herself and put the headcollar on the mare. She wouldn't need any shoes for this. The horse pulled on the halter and swayed from side to side as Verity led her out, and she was nothing like the gentle, reasonable beast Verity knew her as. Verity brought her not to the doors that led to outside, but down another corridor and to the corral, a large circular room fitted with a transparent dome for a ceiling and a mesh floor planted with hydroponic grass. This room was kind of an experiment, but they often put the horses in here, only one at any time, if they were off-colour, and it would have to do for this purpose.

At the sight and smell of the grass, the horse lost interest in her mating urge for a moment, and dropped her head and began ripping up the grass with her teeth, leaving patches of bare gauze behind. Verity unclipped the lead rope from the halter and went back to the stable block, shutting the gate behind her.

She opened the stable door to a cacophony of snorting and stamping. Vladimir stood in the midst of it, looking bewildered.

"What have you done to them?" Verity demanded.

"Nothing!" Vladimir had put the headcollar on the stallion, and the interface on the star on his forehead showed he was synced. He moved restlessly about his loose box, banging his knees against the door. Near the main entrance, the big mare thrust her head out of her stall, ears back, and whinnied. The noises from the other horses lessened somewhat, and the stallion stood still. Verity felt relief that it had not been that mare who had come into season first, for surely there'd be bedlam had that been so.

"Okay," said Verity. "Let's bring him out slowly." She unlocked the door and opened it. The stallion took a leap forward. Vladimir clung on to the rope grimly. The horse backed up and reared, and Vladimir let go and ran inside the stallion's stable, slamming the door behind him. The stallion thundered down the block to the main door and neighed, rearing up again and dropping his forefeet heavily.

"I can't manage this," Vladimir whimpered. "Can't you take him? Please?"

"Oh, all right!" Verity shouted. "You'd better get down to the corral and take control of the mare!" She went to the stallion and reached up, grabbing his headcollar. She managed to get her hand to his implant, and synced him to her. It took all her will to force him down and get him to stand while she opened the door to let Vladimir out to the mare. She stood in the entrance to the block, holding him still, until Vladimir shouted down the corridor that he had the mare.

Verity walked ahead of the stallion, struggling to dominate him with her mind. It was when he saw the gate to the corral that she lost him. He lurched forward and Verity fell on her knees, still gripping the rope. He dragged her forward several paces, his hoofs ringing on the floor not far from her ear, while she repeatedly gave him the thought-prompt to stop. She lost her hold on the rope and he charged forward and jumped the gate into the corral.

"Bloody horse!" Verity cursed as Vladimir ran out, bending over to help her up.

"Are you all right?"

"Of course I'm all right!" When she looked at him, she noticed he was standing awkwardly, his knees bent, trying to conceal a swelling in the crotch of his trousers.

Vladimir went red in the face. "The horses did it."

"What do you mean, horses did it? That's disgusting!"

Vladimir drew his eyebrows down, furrowing his forehead. "You know what I mean!"

"It's just bleedback." Verity got up and headed back towards the corral. "Stop thinking about it and concentrate on controlling the horse." She went to the gate. She didn't know what they would do if the mare decided she wasn't going to co-operate, and attacked the stallion. An angry horse that could not feel fear and a randy horse who was very much afraid sounded like a recipe for disaster.

Inside the corral, the two horses stood, their flanks facing each other, ears twitching. Verity forced down the anger and confusion she was feeling, and tried to broadcast calmness, and feelings of welcome and co-operation. "Don't get into the ring with them," she muttered to Vladimir through gritted teeth. "Whatever happens, stay behind the fence."

Around the barrier of the corral was a walkway, and Vladimir moved along so he was near to the mare. The sound of her blowing air through her nostrils came loud, sounding more like bellows for operating some sort of industrial machinery than the lungs of a living animal. The stallion nickered, and took a step closer. His huge, feathery feet were silent on the carpet of grass, but his weight sent tremors through the hydroponics mesh that Verity sensed through the soles of her boots. Tails swished. The stallion sniffed, his head coming closer to the rear end of the mare.

His muzzle came closer. His lips smacked, and he started to lick greedily under the mare's tail. A rank, musky horse taste filled Verity's mouth, and she couldn't stop herself from grimacing, bringing up saliva and swallowing to try to get rid of the flavour. When she looked at Vladimir, his eyes were shut and he leaned against the wall. Sweat beaded his forehead, and she couldn't make out the expression he was making.

The mare lowered her hindquarters, and a shiver passed over her. With a sudden, crazy burst of maddened excitement, the stallion whirled about and leapt twelve feet in the air, kicking out his hind feet, mane and tail flying. A bloody lust overtook Verity. She could feel how he desired that mare, how her scent maddened him and how he craved every inch of her ebon body. He turned back towards the mare and reared up, tried to mount her sideways on. For an instant Verity forgot where she was standing, and she felt more like the stallion than herself, with the soft, fresh-smelling grass moist against his hoofs. She made him move, taking up position behind the mare, and when he reared up this time, he could come forward, so his sternum landed on the mare's back. She felt him sink in with a tremor that ran through the ligaments in her groin.

As though in a dream, Verity became aware of her own hands on Vladimir's shoulders, of her pushing him to the ground and her mouth pressing against his. The odour of his sweat was rich, like cedarwood, and his skin tasted like insanity.

The stallion was up on the mare, hoofs shuffling and loins quivering, and it was almost over. He backed up and slid off, dropping back down on all fours.

A rich scent of grass filled up her senses. Verity opened her eyes. Through the space under the barriers at the paddock perimeter she could make out eight hoofs. The horses stood in the corral, side to side facing opposite directions like Yin and Yan. Their tails swished across each other's heads as they cropped the grass. They seemed completely unperturbed.

Then she realised she was sitting on top of Vladimir. His face looked like a beetroot with radiation burns, and his shirt was soaked with sweat and hanging open, the buttons ripped off it. He pushed himself up to his elbows, breathing rapidly. "Shit! What just came over me?"

Verity cast about them, suddenly embarrassed and fearful that Sergeant Black or the Commodore might have come in and seen, but they were alone in the corral with the horses. Her mouth opened and closed for several seconds before she managed to get out the word. "*Bleedback!*"

Vladimir looked down at his torn shirt. "Look what you did!" he exclaimed. "How am I supposed to walk across the compound looking like this?"

"Sorry," Verity said, but the feeling she ought to be sincere and show contrition combined with the ridiculousness of the situation made it impossible not to start laughing. She turned away from him, trying to stifle it by covering her hand with her mouth, and gave the thought-prompt to the stallion to come to her. He obeyed. Taking hold of his lead rope, she led him back to the stable block, still laughing. "Put the mare back in her stall."

"So puerile," said Vladimir, but he slunk off as quickly as he could after putting the horses away. Verity went back to her quarters and had a shower and put her sweaty, horse-smelling clothes in the laundry chute. Suddenly she felt more clear-headed than she had done in ages, scrubbing herself briskly and grinning in the shower about the ludicrousness of it all. This was exactly the right state of mind to go through the file fragments the ANT had uncovered.

Most of them had become so corrupted they were illegible.

As Verity searched through them, she began to despair of finding anything useful. Then a mangled signature caught her attention, and her own name farther up in the same document. The hexadecimal fragmentation had caused six out of every sixteen characters to become lost:

A......Cornelian

M......a Order sp......k to opera......Ordered te......ion on sig......e arrest w...... (unlikely ......pond).

Sgt......Verity

Magn......rder membe......etic engin...... project r...... Not known......ssess knowl......f operatio......elligent a......d to influ......Spare if p......e.

Vladimir......hovski

Gene......gineer. Ne......ve and unb......

Commodore ......ith

May sus......omething. ......omes a pro......will appre......

.incerely, ...ron.

Sincerely, Pte Aaron. Verity grinned. Jackpot.

chapter six

VERITY WAS SUPPOSED to have assisted Vladimir with centrifuging the stallion this morning, but he hadn't turned up and the ANT didn't know where he was, and she'd had to take the stallion in by herself. Now she'd come back to the stable, to find the big mare had come into oestrus, and Vladimir still missing with no clue as to his whereabouts.

She left a rude message for him, and then contacted Sergeant Black through the ANT. Verity hated having to ask Sergeant Black for help. From when she'd been first posted to Callisto, Verity had known Sergeant Black didn't like her, perhaps because Verity had been promoted to sergeant and effectively achieved everything Black had done during her career in the Sky Forces at a younger age. She would rather have asked the Commodore to help her, but she couldn't find him either and she still didn't trust him, especially after the ANT had thrown up that scrambled message with his name in it. He'd not turned up at the last meeting Verity had attended .

While she awaited Sergeant Black's arrival, she got the stallion out and took him down to the corral. Away from the smell of mares, he calmed down a little, and ate some grass and rolled on the turf. Verity stared at his glossy barrel-shaped chest and the way he tucked up his legs as he writhed about, enjoying the feel of the grass and the sunlight streaming through the roof. She marvelled at how nature made such lovely creatures, from instructions written in mere purines and pyrimidines that Vladimir could pick and choose amongst, and authored such beastly urges in them to ensure they'd be certain their genes would go on.

"What seems to be the problem?"

Verity turned to meet Sergeant Black, leaning against the load-bearing wall in the entrance to the corral, her fist on her hip and her knee bent, foot balanced on the toe on the wrong side of her other leg in a disdainful posture.

She ignored Black's attitude and tried to explain the situation calmly. "This horse is part of an experimental breeding programme here. The information's on the ANT if you want to look into it. The researcher who's supposed to be running the operation has disappeared, and now the big mare's in oestrus, and if we don't mate them now it's just going to disrupt everything. If you can bring the mare down, I think I can handle him. You just need to keep her under control while they mate."

Sergeant Black made a face, but she turned and went back to the stable block. A few minutes later, she returned with the mare. The stallion whinnied, and Verity took hold of his halter to stop him from escaping while Sergeant Black opened the gate and let the mare inside.

The mare approached the stallion head on, her ears pointed forward, and Verity felt his excitement tempered by a spike of fear. That was a big mare. At close to nineteen hands, she stood almost as tall as the stallion, although not so sturdily built. He started to move away, and she followed, in a nervous chase around the perimeter of the corral. *Stop running*, Verity willed him. *She wouldn't know what to do if she did catch you.* She hoped the mare just wanted to mate, but without being interfaced to her, it was hard to tell. Sergeant Black's face was inscrutable. What if the horses mated, and Verity couldn't control herself again, and she sexually assaulted Sergeant Black? Was it bleedback from her own fear that was making the stallion run?

Verity managed to persuade him to wait. The horses manoeuvred carefully to stand neck to neck, and nosed at one another's shoulders. Slowly, the stallion moved alongside, inevitably towards the mare's back end, and started licking again. Verity grimaced at the taste. There was something that struck her as stealthy and devious about his tactic in this regard. She fancied it was the stallion's own opinion that he was some sort of Lothario with an unusual talent with his tongue. The mare succumbed, lifting her tail and squatting, and he was turning into position and mounting. He entered her, shuffled for thirty seconds, finished, and dropped off. It was a relief once he'd sated his urge, but it left Verity feeling restless and dissatisfied.

"I don't feel too good," said Sergeant Black as the mare came to her. Her pupils were dilated, and a strange expression had taken hold of her face. "I'm going to put this horse away and go and lie down for a bit."

As Verity took the stallion and followed Black and the mare back to the stable block, she checked with the ANT on the location of one Doctor James Standen, with whom she knew Black shared her quarters. He had just left the lab where he worked and was moving towards their billet. *Lie down indeed!* The mare's tail was still up as she walked beside Black, but this didn't seem to interest the stallion, who had reverted back to his placid Doctor Jekyll self, walking obediently beside her.

The horses back in their stalls, Verity stormed down the corridor to her quarters. This was Vladimir's damn research! She hadn't signed up to take on these extra responsibilities, to have her state of mind screwed about and thrown into disarray like this! It had been foisted on her by her employers, and she had accepted it dutifully because that was her work. This was his responsibility, and to shirk his obligations and hide, leaving her to cope with what he couldn't handle alone, that was just utterly irresponsible. More than irresponsible: *aresponsible*, if that was even a word, and if it wasn't then it should be. When she found Vladimir, she was going to... going to... She wanted to give him a piece of her mind. Or did she want to give him more than her mind? Or was all of it just bleedback from the horses?

Vladimir's name had been on that fragmented file she'd found, as had the Commodore's, and she had not been able to find him since the first time she'd looked. What if this was all to do with John Aaron?

In her billet, she switched the computer back on.

My, you're in a strop today! exclaimed Anthony Cornelian's ghost.

Verity picked up the spy's Torrmede card, studying the picture. It didn't match with the glimpse she'd caught of the real man, just before she'd killed him, nor the mangled head she'd seen in Lloyd's lab. She could imagine the owner of the voice in her head shaking out his collar-length hair as he spoke, raising his chin in an imperious sort of way. She put the card down, face up, on the computer, and stuck it there with a length torn off a roll of transparent tape.

My mouth tastes like a horse's arse, she thought as she filled a glass with water.

Why, what have you been doing?

You don't want to know.

Verity downed the water and set the glass on the handbasin. She rubbed her eyes, running her hands over her face. From the bathroom mirror, her reflection stared back at her. In her own face she could see Pilgrennon's sharp, angular nose and Blake's intense, penetrating eyes that she knew so well from the history books. She willed, as she had often done before, for her ancestor's faces to take shape from her visage, to bring her wisdom she had not inherited from them, but they did not. Her face remained her own, and there was a weird tension in it. Her pupils looked much too large for the slight light the sun filled the room with. She needed to find Vladimir.

Back out in the corridor, she came across Lloyd, bounding towards the main entrance and carrying a holdall, a suitcase, a box file, and what appeared to be a telescope folded up in pieces.

"Morning, Sergeant Verity!" he called. "No time to talk today; the lander leaves in five minutes!"

"Have you seen Vladimir or the Commodore today?"

Lloyd frowned. "Not today. I did see the Commodore yesterday. Very busy with something at the moment, though."

Verity found herself staring at him. Her breath seemed very loud all of a sudden. Lloyd was staring back, and he slowly lowered his luggage to the floor. She moved closer, and reached out to him. She had always wanted to run her fingers through that luxuriant coppery mane of his, and now her inhibitions fell away, she found herself finally doing it. It occurred to her that he was exactly her height, and the shape of his body fitted perfectly against hers. When their lips touched he moved slowly in a way that was strangely both calming and maddening. The emotions he broadcast were so precise; so controlled. She sensed from him that he knew exactly what he was doing. He could *play* her like an *instrument* if she'd let him, until she *begged* him to relent. And she wanted that. She'd wanted him for months.

He eased back and relaxed, breaking the vacuum that united their mouths. Verity breathed the smell of him, her lips tingling. "Lloyd, do you know what horses do when they mate?"

Lloyd let out a mercurial chuckle that seemed to resonate deep in Verity's chest. "I can quite imagine," he said, raising an eyebrow and cocking his head to one side, chin down. The way he looked up at her with his soft grey eyes sent an electric charge through her chest.

"Stay here, for a while."

"Ah, *tempus fugit*." Lloyd exhaled through his nose dejectedly. "I'm afraid I can't. The shuttle's leaving soon. I have to shift this stuff." He picked up his things.

"Quickly?" Verity suggested.

Lloyd shook his head. "No, really. I have to leave. There's always time when I come back. You've not seen the station before, have you? You'll have to come up there with me one time." He waved an arm to the view of Jupiter through the window. "I'll see you on the first quarter."

"See you in eight days."

"*Ave et vale*," Lloyd called over his shoulder as he bounded away down the corridor with his luggage.

It was going to be a long eight days. She'd have to find something to read, to pass the time. Verity didn't want to look for Vladimir any more. After Lloyd, he would be too much of an anticlimax. That would be like turning down steak in order to eat... levigated esculents. She supposed she had better at least go through some sort of procedure. He couldn't possibly have been in the centrifuge, because she'd been there that morning and she'd not seen him, and someone would have complained to her if he'd ignored the booking procedure. The only other place she could think of where he might have gone was outside. She supposed she ought to go to the tower and use the surveillance telescopes there.

She went to the observation block and ascended the narrow spiral staircase, feet ringing on the thin metal steps. At the top, windows all around the room's circumference offered a 360 view of the ice plains.

She immediately looked down, checking around the base of the compound. She couldn't see anyone within the gates. Scanning the plain, she couldn't see anything out of the usual there either.

A bright star moved against the dimmer ones still visible in the sky. That was Lloyd's shuttle, taking him up to the main station. There was the main station itself, another bright star as it passed through conjunction with Callisto on its orbit around Jupiter. Verity trained one of the telescopes on it, although it revealed little detail, looking like a reflective metal shaving rather than a star. The shuttle did have some definition to it when she looked. She made out the shape of the fuselage and the long stream of hot gases from its fusion engine.

She let the telescope wander down, until its aperture brought unfocused jagged shapes into view. Verity turned the focus knob until they resolved into ice protrusions on the top of the cliff at the scarp. Vladimir wouldn't have gone to the scarp, would he? What could he possibly do there? Why would he possibly want to go anywhere outside the base? It didn't make sense.

The roving telescope view lit upon something unfamiliar in the landscape of sharp gleaming needles. Some black object draped among the stands of ice on the steep decline down the cliff. With a sharp intake of breath, she recognised it as a horse — dead, obviously. None of the horses were out. It had to be the horse John Aaron had taken. She moved the barrel of the telescope frantically, searching for another body. There it was, a pathetic shape, run through the chest by the spiny palisade he'd fallen upon. Verity increased the magnification and adjusted the focus on the face. The hands were still bound together. The face — it was still recognisable. Private Aaron.

He must have fallen to his death. He wasn't synced to the horse. It would be so easy for him to lose control, being unable to communicate danger to an animal unable to feel fear.

Verity stepped away from the telescope. So he had never gone anywhere else. She'd told him to return the horse and he'd fallen and they'd both died. The situation was of his own making, and she'd had to make a decision quickly. It had been the right decision, or so Commodore Smith had told her. She checked the ANT again, and found a note had been attached to Vladimir Bolokhovski's name:

Recalled to Torrmede regarding business/ research.

He wasn't missing. He'd just had to go back at short notice for whatever reason. No doubt he'd been on the same shuttle that had taken Lloyd up. Slowly, Verity made her way back down and to her cabin. Inconsiderate of him not to tell her, to leave her in the lurch, picking up the pieces of his horse breeding project.

Anthony Cornelian's computer still lay on her desk. *You*

seem on edge.

Verity threw herself down on the bed, ignoring Anthony Cornelian's ghost. She tried to imagine how Lloyd Farron would look with his shirt torn open and his bare chest exposed.

Hell, no, don't be disgusting.

Bleedback. It works both ways. *What, you don't think Farron's sexy, but you do think Vladimir and Sergeant Black are? You have no taste.*

What happened to you?

Verity had no idea if interacting with Cornelian's personality imprint would make it any more or less likely she'd be able to extract any useful information from the computer, but she didn't see any harm in it. After all, he wasn't coming back for it, and anyone else who tried to get anything off it would be in the same position she was. *I'm frustrated because the horses mated and I tried it on with Farron and I thought for a moment I'd be able to get off with him, but he's gone off to the main station instead.*

I could sort that for you, if I still had hands. I'm good with my hands.

Ghosts are supposed to be morose and mournful, and haunt the living, not perv on them. Verity reached over and picked up the printout of the file fragments from yesterday. If John Aaron had written it and John Aaron was now dead and no-one had noticed, who could there have been that he'd sent it to? She gazed at the partial signature on the bottom. Not the Commodore, who was still disappeared, because his name was mentioned on the list of people along with Vladimir's and her own. Unless that was a deliberate decoy.

Her fingers tightened on the paper. Unless it wasn't Aaron's name... Anthony's disgust at her fantasy suddenly resurfaced in her mind. It wasn't *Pte Aaron*, it was *Ir Farron*. Inquisitor Lloyd Farron.

Verity quickly got to her feet, facing the computer. *What do you know about Farron? It's him you were sent here to spy on, isn't it?*

Ah, so you do have some skills of deduction. You're not just a pretty face.

Verity felt a sudden annoyance. *You are dead because of something to do with this. The Magnolia Order is involved, and I'm trying to help you and all you do is act like a letch!*

Farron is dangerous. You need to keep out of this.

Look, the Magnolia Order sent you here, didn't they? I'm with the Magnolia Order. Doesn't that mean we're on the same side and we've to help each other?

I know you're with the Magnolia Order. They warned me about you.

What? Stop pissing about, this is serious. Vladimir's missing and so's the Commodore.

Vladimir? The cute young chap with the Russian accent? The one writing the thesis? There came a pause in Anthony's transmission, and the voice in Verity's head carried worry and caution when it continued. *What's his thesis in? Please don't tell me he was a genetic engineer.*

chapter seven

*N*OW JUST HOLD ON. *What do you think you're doing?*

Verity finished snapping the buckles on her armour, tightened her katana belt, and shoved the computer with Anthony's ghost on it into the bag with the other things. *I'm going to break into Farron's lab and find out what the hell's going on. There must be some clues in there.*

When I said the Magnolia Order warned me about you, I meant they warned me not to get you involved. They considered cutting you in and asking you to act as an inside agent, but they decided you were too young and you didn't have enough experience, and the risk to you would be too high. They also warned me that you were likely to be the biggest danger to the mission asides from Farron himself. I wasn't given orders for this contingency. Let's stop and discuss this.

Verity put her hand on the hilt of her katana as she walked towards the horse block. *Well, that's just tough, because I am involved now, and I'm going to get to the bottom of this, and I'm going to tell the Magnolia Order what I think of them for dismissing me as* young *and* inexperienced! *If you've got something to tell me, you can tell it to me now!*

Look, I'll try to tell you what I know, but it's not a lot. Farron is up to something. He's abusing his inquisitors' privileges and he's planning something out here. Finding out what it was he was plotting evidently got me killed. If you go barging into Farron's lab, you're going to end up with an arrest warrant on yourself, and then where will that get us?

You think I haven't thought of that? Verity irrupted into the stables. Horses snorted and stamped in response to the anger she was broadcasting. She checked every box to be sure no-one hid in them, before syncing herself to one of the horses and tacking it up. She grabbed a bore kit from the store cupboard and bundled it into the bag on the horse, and fitted a long-range transmitter to the horse's head armour over its implant. After leading the horse out into the courtyard, she gave the signal to it to run to a landmark fifteen miles away and then return to the ANT's beacon. The horse raced away, through the main gates and into the glare of the sun. Verity watched its dark shape dwindling away on the immense black plain. *There. Now everyone thinks I'm outside doing boring samples.* She dropped the bag from her shoulders and pulled out a roll of gaffer tape and a piece of metal foil.

You know, maybe the Magnolia Order underestimated you, Anthony thought. *But then again, I've never known the Magnolia Order to be wrong before, so you're bound to do something stupid that'll vindicate them in a moment.*

Oh ha ha very funny, Verity returned. *Let's go and burgle Farron's lab before that horse comes back.* She folded the foil into a piece a few inches square, and taped it to her forehead over her implant, hiding her signal from the ANT.

Mounted on the door outside Farron's lab was a security lock with a steady red light on it. Farron alone would know the thought-prompt to open it.

Anthony Cornelian must have had some kind of device to break in with. She was incommunicado with her neural shunt insulated, and couldn't ask the computer in her bag without exposing her location to the ANT. That plastic thing she'd found on the body, perhaps. She found it in her bag. It looked like some sort of electronic skeleton key, so she stuck it in the security lock and turned it. The door slid back into its wall recess.

Verity stepped inside. She scanned the lab with her back to the wall. With her implant covered she was blind to any signal that might help her search or alert her to danger.

She pulled open a drawer. Electronics things: wires and stuff that were meant to be connected to people's interfaces to put currents through their brains and short-circuit their mental wiring. Verity shoved the drawer closed again. Her eyes wandered, almost without thinking, to take in the chair — similar to the type in dental surgeries, but with a harness like in the seat of a fighter jet, and thick straps where the wrists and ankles would go.

She pulled open another drawer. Syringes and needles, all neatly lined up and wrapped in sterile plastic. On the table, a few slates and bits of computer equipment. Lab coats hanging on a peg. At the back of the room, on the wall perpendicular to the broad windows occupying the far wall, there was a closed door. What lay behind that? Probably just a store room and a fridge for keeping drugs in. Verity found herself staring at it, and although she felt no signals, an odd feeling began to creep over her.

Verity shook her head. This was irrational. It must just be an effect of being deprived of signals, like little kids were frightened of the dark because they couldn't see what it hid. Yet still she feared opening that door. The doorknob turned smoothly when she tried it, and the catch clicked and the door swung back.

The smell and the hum of a machine hit her first, and then she saw the wires snaking all over the table, the machine under the bench and the plastic tubes bringing dark fluid to and fro through two ports in the front of it. The head hadn't been disposed of as Farron had asserted. It was still on the table, still connected to the machinery, although the skin had started to turn grey, and the wound in the neck had started to fester without a proper immune system to stave off infection. As she stared at it, the eye that was still functional opened, its pupil swivelling towards her. The head beheld her, its expression dour and immobile.

Nausea welled up, and Verity's mouth filled with saliva. She swallowed, trying to force it down, stopping herself from vomiting. He'd been in this not-quite dead state ever since she'd cut him down on the scarp. Why had Farron done this?

This didn't match up with the man she knew.

Yet this version of Anthony Cornelian, or what was left of him, must know what was going on. And she needed that information. After a moment, she slid the bag off her shoulders and opened it.

"You're Anthony Cornelian," she addressed the head. "I'm Zeta Verity. I killed you... I was following orders. I didn't realise who you were and what was going on. I can't change that back, but I'm going to try to put it right. The only thing I can give you now is mercy. I'm going to make Farron pay for what he's done."

Verity paused, but the expression on the face did not change. She continued. "You can't talk, 'cause you've got no lungs, and I can't get the information from your mind because I'm not an inquisitor." Verity reached into the bag and brought out the computer. "But you can transfer the data to your computer, and I swear to you this will end now, and that I'll give everything I've got in me to make sure it reaches the Magnolia Order and Lloyd Farron is stopped."

Verity held out the computer. The head remained staring at her, and then it blinked. The processing light on the slate started to flash. After the flickering had stopped, the head closed its eye.

Verity put the slate back in the bag. She didn't know if the data had been transferred successfully. She couldn't interface with the computer to check, but she had made an oath, and she would show the living death of Anthony Cornelian that there were people left in the Solar System capable of honour.

Her hand landed on the hilt of her katana. Her feet found their position and the steel rushed from the sheath into a sweeping strike with the full force of her body behind it. The head on the table exploded, hurling reanimation fluid and pieces of brain and skull up the wall. The readouts on the monitors went haywire.

Verity hefted the bag back onto her shoulders as she retreated outside, wiping her katana savagely on Lloyd Farron's lab coat before resheathing it.

The piercing wail of the emergency alarm sent her flying for the door. Verity ran from the lab and hid in a side corridor, flattening herself behind a first aid cupboard. Boots rang on the floor, and voices shouted, then people were in the lab. "It's Sergeant Verity." That was Sergeant Black's voice. "The ANT says she's out with one of the horses. Quickly, let's get after her." Footsteps again, this time retreating to the stables. She stayed put, trying to keep her breathing steady, until she was sure they'd gone.

She crept down the corridor in the other direction, keeping her shoulder close to the wall and her hand on her katana. She passed the habitation block and chanced a look into the corridor leading to her billet. The door had already been forced open, and sounds of a search emanated from within. She had to stay away from the stables long enough for Sergeant Black to get away, but not so long that Sergeant Black caught up with the decoy horse and saw the trick and came back. She had no idea how long that would be.

She went back to the stables the long way round. Listening carefully outside, she heard nothing from within, apart from a horse crunching its feed. She slipped through the door and hid behind an open stable door, before peering over it and checking. All clear. All the horses were gone. Everyone who could ride must be out hunting her. Just the stallion, whom she'd heard eating from outside, remained.

The new tack she'd ordered for him had arrived by now, and it stood on the rack outside his stable. It had never been used before. This horse had not been broken in, and he was not fearless like the mares she was used to. He was unpredictable and untried, yet there were no other horses. She would get nowhere on foot. If there was even anywhere to go.

Verity ripped off the tape on her forehead. *Anthony?*

Anthony!

For what seemed like a long time, he didn't respond.

Anthony!

I've decided I'm going to help you. His voice came at last, sorrowful and despondent in her thoughts.

Verity opened the stallion's stable door, synced him to her, and picked up the saddle. *We need to get out of here, quickly! Where were you going when I killed you on the scarp?* She readied the horse to the idea of a weight being placed on his back, and put the saddle on, quickly fastening the girth. He turned his head to get a better view and stood awkwardly, but didn't start panicking.

Can you fly?

I'm a sergeant in the Sky Forces! Of course I can fly!

There's a lander. I hid it. I think I can direct you to it once we get moving.

Verity put on the rest of the armour and the shoes on the horse. She dug her helmet out of the food bin where she'd concealed it, and dusted it off before putting it on. The inside of it smelt of horse food.

Now came the difficult part. She led the stallion out of his stall. She had to jump to get up on his back, and he started. Verity reassured him, but already her heart was pumping faster than it should, and a clammy sweatiness lined her gloves. She was afraid, and he was afraid, and the only purpose it served was to propagate a feedback loop in which they made one another more scared. She tried to fight back the fear, reassuring the horse that he was safe with her. As she squirmed her knees to seat herself firmly in the saddle, he flicked out his back legs, not liking the alien, alarming sensation of having something pressing onto his body.

Verity tested her weight in the stirrups, and picked up the reins. Neither would be much use, since he'd never been trained for them. She'd have to do this on thought-prompts alone.

She gave the command for him to move forward, and he obeyed. His walking pace was still far too bouncy, though. Verity told herself, or rather she hoped, that he'd feel much more natural as soon as they were out and galloping. Out they rode through the main door, the noise of his hoofs ringing loudly from the walls in the space of the corridor. She urged him faster as they went through the compound's main gate, up through bouncing trot to rolling canter, and into full gallop. He did ease into a better pace after that, she was relieved to find. Verity set her sights on the lighter edge of the scarp in the distance, a few miles away. Jupiter formed a perfect semicircle, and the ice sparkled in the sun.

The stallion didn't like the cold air in his lungs. He snorted clouds like a steam engine as he galloped. *You're nearly as much of a wimp as Vladimir*, she thought fondly to him. As she began to adjust to him, she started to enjoy the novelty of riding a different horse to the mares. He felt wider between her knees, and his unclipped mane flew from his neck with his speed, his breath freezing on it and turning it to whippy dreadlocks.

In the horse's vision she saw shapes moving against the dark plain, racing between the blunted spires. Horses. Sergeant Black's squadron. They'd caught up with the decoy horse, and now they were coming back for her. Verity gave the thought-prompt to the stallion for all the speed he could give. She felt his pace quicken, but he didn't feel as fast as the big mare did, the horse she recognised Sergeant Black riding in the distance. The chasing horses were curving round, coming to intercept their path, their strides elongated and greyhound-like in the low gravity. Already Verity was picking up strange things from the stallion's feedback. There was way too much adrenaline in his system. If this had been one of the mares, she'd be seriously concerned.

She could see the jagged stands of ice protruding from

the rise of the cliff. She recalled the way she'd gone up there, when she'd chased Anthony. Over the top was quickest, and she knew Sergeant Black wasn't all that familiar with the scarp, and she was unlikely to know the ascent and trust her horse like Verity did.

She slowed the horse as they closed in, fixed focus on the first point she needed him to jump to, and gave the thought-prompt.

Doubt and panic rushed into his mind from nowhere. He shied, halting and suddenly rearing up. Verity had been anticipating the motion of the jump, and nearly lost her seat. She fell forward on his neck and lost precious seconds recovering her balance before she could regain control, pressing the stallion on towards the track around the edge of the cliff. Hoofbeats sounded behind her.

"Zeta Verity, I have a warrant for your arrest! Halt in the name of the Meritocracy!"

Verity could see Black leaning forward from her horse, reaching for her. "Sergeant Black!"

Sergeant Black reached to her hip, for a weapon, the mare so close her head was almost touching the stallion's hindquarters.

Do something! In the back of her mind, Verity felt a sudden *deja vu* from Anthony. She at once gave two thought-prompts: one to the stallion's cybernetic armour that caused the grip crampons to extend from his shoes, and the other to him to lash out with his hind feet. She felt the powerful kick connect, and the mare's scream was hideous to her ears. Sergeant Black overbalanced and fell. As the stallion ran up the incline into the forest of ice, Verity saw her curled in a foetal position in his vision, other horses pulling away and trying to step over her. The mare... at least she was on her feet, although she'd stopped running. That she'd had to do that to a horse she knew, she cared about, and that might be pregnant... she'd never forgive herself if it turned out the big mare had to be shot.

She tried to put what had happened out of her mind, and concentrated on navigating the path ahead. Ice spikes rushed past, and now she understood the adrenaline in the horse's blood was at least doing something. His fear of what was chasing him outweighed any apprehension he had about the path and the unknown territory ahead. It was fear that pushed him faster, putting his hoofs where a fearless horse's rider might hesitate before risking.

The stallion rounded the side of the scarp, and they raced along the path she and Vladimir had come, where she'd climbed down to Anthony Cornelian's body. Ice flashed in the sun ahead of the stallion's broad neck, his mane flying and icy vapours rushing from his nostrils with every jarring stride.

Anthony, where is it?

It's not far. It's just at the edge of that big crater.

Tell me when! A horse had appeared on the path close behind, and it was gaining on her.

I'm not sure.

When will you be sure? Verity turned her head for a better view of the crater, but she could see only the ice barbs of the brink, and far away the opposite wall. If she jumped too soon, they'd end up in the crater, and the fall would kill both her and the stallion. It suddenly occurred to her that Sergeant Black might kill her, find the computer in her bag, realise what was going on as she had, and try to flee to the lander. Then someone else would kill *her* and the cycle would repeat. At this moment, her own mortality seemed risible. She hadn't got out of bed this morning expecting to end up here. She hadn't thought she would die this day.

I think it's here.

Are you sure?

No.

"Damn!" Verity looked to the edge of the scarp, sizing up the jump. If he refused, it would be game over. If Anthony was wrong and that was crater below and not the plateau, it would be game over. She focussed on her interface with the horse. She could not know doubt. There was too much fear in him for her to have that margin. She concentrated, visualising the plateau just below the edge and the easy drop, the straightforward landing. As she gave the thought-prompt to jump, she was utterly sure of her conviction.

The stallion pushed off with his hindquarters. His forelegs tucked up into the leap, his head dropping to look forward. The length of his back tensed, stabilising him in midair as they soared over the ridge. The plateau lay twenty feet below, just as she had imagined it.

His forelegs stretched out to meet the ice, and Verity leaned forward into the saddle for the landing. After a few paces, he came to a stop.

Where's the lander?

It's behind you, under the ledge!

Verity kicked her feet loose and dismounted. It would take a moment for her pursuers to get down here. They'd probably have to stop and dismount and look over the edge to make sure they weren't following her to their deaths. Quickly she reached up the the stallion's head and desynced from him. She'd have to hope the other riders would catch him and take him home.

She ran back to where the cliff would hide her, and where she saw a white shape nestled among boulders and shadows at the foot of the scarp. She felt very small and low down without the horse under her, and although she was racing to it in great leaps, her speed was pathetic and insignificant compared to the horse's.

She reached the lander, and in her peripheral vision she saw a shape fly over high above. The horses were leaping down, but they saw the stallion and chased after him as soon as their hoofs hit the ice. Their riders must not have thought to check their horses' vision, for if they had they would have seen an anomalous pale form standing out against the dusty ice.

The lander's domed white shape was made primarily from a fusion engine surrounded by high-pressure tanks to hold supercritical hydrogen. The cabin comprised only the foremost fifth of the thing. Its short delta wing lay flattened close to the ground, making it look like a huge limpet.

What's the thought-prompt for it?

Anthony conveyed it, and when she relayed it to the lander, the door unlocked. She hurried to turn the wheel that would release the seal. The cabin within was not much warmer than the outside temperature. There were only two seats, one behind the other. Verity spun the wheel to seal the door. She dumped her helmet in the back seat and stuffed the bag with Anthony in it down the footwell. She landed heavily in the pilot's seat and wrestled the harness over her shoulders, snapping the buckle shut.

Hitting the ignition switch sent a trickle of hydrogen into the fusion engine. Warm, dry air rushed up from grilles at the bottom of the cockpit. Verity couldn't manage the controls with her gloves on, but when she took them off, the steering bar was still burning cold.

The surface surrounding the lander was uneven, strewn with lumps of ice and broken pieces from the scarp above. *How am I supposed to take off in this thing? There's no runway!*

It's got a gyromagnetic levitator, like the gyromags the Stormraiders use back on Earth and Mars. It skims over the surface, like a hovercraft. You need to start the cryomagnet to take off.

Verity flicked up the switch marked *cryomagnet*. A dull hum became audible. Outside the reinforced panes of vitreous alloy that made up the forward window, a horse and rider appeared in the distance. Others followed close behind. They had seen the lander.

The pitch of the hum grew until it reached a steady level, and a green light above the cryomagnet switch came on.

Plasma thrust online, quickly! Anthony told her.

Verity found the plasma thrust switch and hit it. The craft rose slowly as the plasma thrusters forced charged particles into the magnetic field beneath its keel. The lander felt wobbly and unsteady on its frictionless cushion of ions. She put the main fusion engine online, and there came a whoosh of something depressurising followed by a roar of fusion. The force flung her back against her seat and the scabrous landscape rushed past below. Verity gripped the steering bar to counter the instability the acceleration through the atmosphere generated, gradually pushing it down to raise the craft's nose and gain altitude. The horses scattered. As the ground fell away, the craggy features of the ice became smooth and indistinct, and the curve of the horizon became apparent.

As the G-force eased away from her back and neck, Callisto appeared as a scratched indigo ovoid outlined by the glowing azure arc of its atmosphere.

An image appeared on the lander's screen: a map of Callisto and Jupiter with various orbital lines around it, and a dashed line delineating a course. Verity sensed the pull of an adjusting force. *Hey, it's playing silly buggers.*

It's just the autopilot moving into course to intercept the yacht.

Yacht?

My yacht, the one the lander belongs to.

You've got a yacht orbiting here? How come no-one noticed?

No-one looked. Anthony's voice carried a current of amusement.

As Verity watched the schematic, a bright star appeared in the front window.

There it is. Prepare to dock.

chapter eight

AS THE STAR in the lander's front window grew brighter, it began to take form. Verity recognised the bulk of a fusion engine at the stern, and forward of that a centrifuge collar, lit by its sharp albedo. Around the forward part, just back of the prow, articulated metal limbs were retracted in close, like the spokes of a furled umbrella.

The straps pressed into Verity's shoulders as the ship's autopilot commenced braking thrust. *Never thought I'd see it again*, said Anthony's voice in the back of her mind.

The yacht loomed in the forward window. A stream of gas gushed across the edge of the window as the carbon dioxide ballast activated. The front of the lander began to rotate away from the yacht, bringing it in to line with a lander-shaped slot on the underside of the larger vessel. All thrust had ceased, and the craft moved slowly in to dock. Gases hissed through the lander's walls. The edge of the yacht's recess gradually descended over the lander's window, covering the view of the stars and Callisto below.

A click and a loud ping conducted through the hull. A green symbol lit up on the hatch above her head.

Verity unfastened her seatbelt and pushed up from her chair. She had to brace her feet against the wall in order to turn the wheel and open the hatch, revealing a white corridor. She pulled herself back down by the headrest of the pilot's seat, pulling the bag with Anthony in it out of the footwell and picking up her helmet.

She bent her knees, setting her feet to the chair and aiming her head into the corridor above. She pushed up and drifted into the yacht, grabbing one of the wall rungs to stop herself from crashing into the locker at the far end of the corridor. She jammed her helmet in it and took off the rest of her armour, which was already impeding her in this weightless environment.

Shoving the Anthony bag ahead of her, she made her way fore and into the yacht's cabin. She found a fairly spartan room, with just two chairs and a bank of controls on a sloping console facing the broad front window. The rear wall bore four hinged seats, two either side of the door, with seatbelts. The cockpit had been personalised with a number of holographs and drawings affixed to the walls at the window's edges. One of them showed a man she matched to the image on Anthony's Torrmede card, he grinning and with his arm draped over the shoulder of another man with dark hair, also grinning.

Verity studied the smile, the wavy caramel-coloured hair, trying to overwrite the memory of the mutilated head with a model of the man he had been in life.

Verity's eyes wandered to a pencil drawing. It depicted a shirtless man from behind, with a sinuous, lean back, narrow buttocks, and long legs. From the style of his hair, it looked like he was the other man in image with Anthony. *He your boyfriend?*

No.

Who's he?

His name's Jay Tourmaline.

You draw these? Verity glanced at the pictures, many of them showing the same man, and others showing different men or women, mostly in states of undress that might be optimistically described as artistic. A short, chubby woman with an alluring grin, short-cropped hair, and big, bright eyes, the hollows of her collarbone and the dimples around the edges of her wide areolae picked out with careful shading; a tattooed, pigeon-chested man with facial piercings; an enormously fat man smiling and reclining on his back with his legs wide open, private parts looking comically small against the expansive flesh folds of his body.

Yes.

They're very skilful. But you really do have a dirty mind.

I'm going to need you to send a message to Torrmede.

Verity turned from Anthony's artwork to the consoles spreading before the bridge windows. *Saying what?*

Never mind that. Torrmede's almost at direct opposition to Jupiter right now. It's going to take 56 minutes for the transmission to reach them. Let's get the request sent and I'll go over it with you what it is you need to tell them while we wait two hours for the response to come back.

Two hours! Isn't there a quicker way?

Unless you know of some way of circumventing Einstein's laws, no there isn't.

Verity pulled herself down into a chair. *Okay. What do I do?*

You'll need to open the sail in order to power up the transmitter.

Sail?

Of course it's got a sail. It's a yacht, isn't it? Only it's a sun-yacht, so it's got a photosail.

Of course. Verity remembered the retracted machinery she'd seen around the forward part of the hull. A reflective sail for generating motion from the radiation pressure of the sun. She studied the controls. In the centre of the console was a transparent bubble with what looked like a compass inside it, only this compass was octahedral and mounted on gimbals, with six points labelled NESWUD. The panel for the sail was to the right: a lever and a few dials and unlit symbols. She pushed the lever, and one of the symbols illuminated. Whirrs and clicks started up, transmitted through the metal of the hull.

Don't touch anything until the green light comes on, Anthony admonished. *It's a delicate piece of machinery and the wires will become detuned if you try to operate the mirrors or the photovoltaics before it's fully open.*

I'm not a moron, you know, Verity answered.

Possibly not. But I'm not going to take the risk with my sun-yacht.

What do you care about your sun-yacht anyway? You're dead and it's not like you'll be sailing into the sunset in it when all this is over.

Perhaps not, but I didn't intend for it to be manhandled by some thug from the Sky Forces. I've left very specific instructions in my will regarding this sun-yacht, and when you've finished borrowing it for the purposes of the mission, I want it returned to its rightful owner undamaged!

Verity pushed herself back against the chair, feet against the edge of the console, and exhaled. Outside the window, the limbs of the photosail were beginning to extend, telescoping outwards and unfolding. Lines of hypertensile cables threaded with mirrors strung between the struts, giving the sail the appearance of a spider's web

The noise of the motors ceased, and the green light came up on the control panel. Verity removed her feet and leaned over to the controls. *Now what?*

You need to set the auto tracker for the photovoltaics. The radiotransmitter will take a few minutes to build up enough charge.

Verity studied the controls and worked out what she needed to change fairly quickly. The cables connecting the reflective plates to the struts began to move, rotating the mirrors to the sun to harvest its light. They scattered some of the light upon the bridge windows, filling the room with a mellow glow.

So, Verity settled herself back into the chair as best she could in the absence of gravity. *What is it Farron's doing, and what's this data you stole?*

Farron is using his skills as an inquisitor to brainwash and hypnotise the personnel of the Callisto base.

Verity squinted, trying to make sense of this. *For what end?*

That's what the Magnolia Order sent me to find out. He's trying to execute a coup. He's making a bid for autonomous rule on Callisto.

What? Verity's frown deepened. *He can't do that. It won't work. For a province to be given autonomous rule, the electorate there have to vote it in, and that's never happened before. How does he expect he can stand against the Meritocracy?*

It's precisely right that the local electorate have to nominate and vote in autonomy. The voice in the back of Verity's mind was grave. *The population of the base on Callisto is small, only a few hundred staff and researchers. If he can get roughly half the populace, including some of the higher-ranking meritocrats on side to nominate autonomy, and then vote for it on referendum day, he's got himself autonomous rule. That's what I discovered. That's why a warrant was issued on me.*

Verity stared at the control bank and the bright dappled pattern the photosail formed around the windows. *But if he pulls off a coup, and the Meritocracy realises how he's done it, all that will happen is that the Spokesmen will veto it, or the Electorate will nominate something to do with it and vote it through next referendum day, and then the Meritocracy will launch an invasion on Callisto and reclaim the base. It would be stupid to attempt a coup.*

There's something more. Something I wasn't able to uncover before I was exposed. A number of high profile genetic engineers have gone missing over the last year. All the evidence points at Farron. He's doing something in genetic research, and it's almost certainly illegal. My guess is he's raised some sort of genetically augmented army to fight for him. The Magnolia Order thought it was on Callisto. I've been there and I'm sure it's not. It must be somewhere else.

Vladimir, Verity realised. *The Jupiter orbital station. Farron goes there every half local day, when its orbit comes into conjunction with Callisto.*

The radiotransmitter is ready. Let's send the message now, and discuss this later.

Okay. Verity found the panel for the radio. An orbital schematic came up when she activated it, allowing her to program it to automatically target and track Torrmede with the antenna. *What do I need to send?*

Just put what I told you into a standard distress call. You're the one with the military background. I'll tell you if there's anything you miss.

Verity leaned over so her mouth was close to the mic. "Mayday, mayday. This is Sergeant Verity of the Sky Forces Research Branch calling MANTIcore of Torrmede. This message is a Class One distress call and is for the attention of the Spokesmen of the Meritocracy... and..." Anthony was requesting she add something. "Takahashi Tōru of the Magnolia Order. I report a crisis on Callisto and require backup and instructions to deal with a potential coup orchestrated by Inquisitor Lloyd Farron. I require a Freedom of Information exemption override and information on the whereabouts of Vladimir Bolokhovski who works at the genetic research department of the University on the grounds of suspicion of his life being at risk. Over."

That's it recorded. Now transmit it.

Verity pressed the button to send the message. A light blinked twice, indicating it had been successful. She closed her eyes and pushed back against the chair, becoming aware of the ache in her muscles and the smell of sweat and horse on her clothing. The null gravity was starting to give her a headache and make her nose stuffy. She hadn't eaten since that morning, and the ache of hunger was starting to claw at her stomach.

Why don't we get some food and go to the centrifuge? Anthony suggested. *There's some space adaptation remedy medicine in the kitchen, too.*

Verity pulled herself over the back of the chair and pushed

towards the door. *Where is it?*

Just through there. The door on the right's a lavatory and a shower.

The kitchen turned out to be a smallish room, with appliances and cupboards built into all five walls surrounding the central space. Verity stabilised herself against a grip rung and pulled open the fridge door. Packets of stuff filled drawers and elastic pockets strapped to the inside of the door. *You've got real cheese? And meat!*

I've got wine, too!

I don't drink alcohol. It impairs reactions and judgment.

Your loss.

Verity found the medicine and took some of it, washing it down with a bottle of water filled from a tap sticking out of the wall by the door. *I want to have a shower first.*

Okay, so long as you don't leave hair in the soap or towels floating around.

What are you going to do if I do?

Spank you. And enjoy it.

Pervert.

The shower-room turned out to be rather small, with a shower-head on a hose and ventilation grids on opposite walls, along with a fan-assisted toilet in one corner vertex. Verity stripped off in the corridor and left her dirty clothes there. When she started the shower, a fan began to operate, causing a wind to blow from one grid to the other and pulling the stream of water down with it.

Shut the door so the water doesn't go into the corridor, Anthony told her.

She pulled the door closed and wriggled under the spray, holding on to a rail and turning about so the stream ran over her. She wet her hair and spat out the water that had got into her mouth and nose. *Shut up*, she thought, sensing the feeling in the back of her mind that she was beginning to recognise as Anthony's sexual curiosity.

I didn't say anything!

Verity found a soap-on-a-rope leashed to a rail and drifting, and rubbed it in her hands to make a lather. *I'm gonna turn you off*, she warned Anthony.

You keep threatening to turn me off, said Anthony, *but all you do is turn me on.*

If ghosts that throw stuff around are called poltergeists, what are ghosts that are voyeurs called? Verity soaped her crotch and armpits.

Men? Anthony suggested. *You should enjoy your body while you can. Some day, you might not have one.*

Sorry about that, Verity thought. *Pineapple and passionfruit shampoo and conditioner?* she chided, reading the label of the container hooked on the rail beside the soap.

It smells nice. And it's good for my hair! Hey, don't use loads! That's expensive shit!

Verity washed her hair in Anthony's fancy shampoo, and switched off the shower. The extractor fan seemed to have pulled most of the water out of the air. She squeezed her wet hair and shook it out. The medicine was starting to kick in on her headache, and the warm damp air in the shower had started to clear her nose.

How are you liking my sun-yacht anyway?

Verity considered. *It doesn't offer much in the way of privacy.* She picked up the bag from the corridor. *Let's see this centrifuge, then.*

She gathered together some cheese and biscuits with some packets of meat and chocolate, and a carton of fruit juice from the fridge in the kitchen. She had to stuff them inside the bag so she didn't drop them in the corridor.

The centrifuge operated much like the ones on the base on Callisto, but contained four awkwardly shaped rooms at right angles to one another. A dressing gown, a pair of slippers, and a duvet floated in the bedroom, but they drifted into the wall and sank to the floor when Verity closed the hatch and switched the centrifuge on. The weight pressing her feet to the floor slowly increased. Verity gathered up the duvet and threw it back on the bed. She tipped the contents of the bag out and set Anthony's computer down at the corner of the mattress. She pulled on the dressing gown, made from a scratchy woolly fabric. Its material enclosed an unfamiliar male scent that made her wonder again about the real man Anthony had been. Did he wake every morning and pull on this dressing gown? Perhaps he yawned, and stretched, and smiled and ran fingers through hair.

Verity arranged the cheeses and the grapes on a board. She cut a thick wedge of Lunar Blue and squashed it on a biscuit.

Nothing like good cheese, Anthony thought as she chewed it.

She glanced up at the windows on either corner of the ceiling. Stars drifted past with the rotation of the centrifuge.

There's a thought-prompt to make the windows turn to mirrors.

Verity swallowed. *That's just not right, having mirrors where you sleep.*

Probably not, but if I lie in bed and see the stars turn over a few dozen times, I start to feel like I'm going to throw up.

For a while, neither of them formed any conscious thoughts, and Verity ate and enjoyed it, and Anthony savoured the taste of the food through her senses.

How long until we hear back from Torrmede?

Not for another fifty minutes at least.

You need to tell me everything you know about what's going on.

Zeta, Farron is dangerous. The Magnolia Order don't want you involved in this.

Verity threw a pillow at the wall. *And you can stop calling me Zeta! That's not my name, it's just a number!*

Sorry.

She pulled Anthony Cornelian's bedcover over herself and closed her eyes. Even though she'd never known him, his smell on the bed seemed familiar and not unpleasant. If they'd met properly, in real life, she might have liked him a lot, perhaps as much as Gecko. Especially when since he'd been flesh and blood, she wouldn't have been aware of all the lewd thoughts he had in the privacy of his own head.

I'd have liked to have drawn you, Anthony concurred.

I don't think I could keep still long enough, Verity thought. *So what is the Magnolia Order anyway? Who's in charge of it? Who are they to say I'm not to get involved?*

I don't know who's in charge of it. And even if I did, I wouldn't be able to tell you. I took an oath. They have a hierarchy system that determines who's allowed to know what. You're rather like an affiliate member, which means you have potential and they'll tell you more when you're ready to know more.

What about Farron? What are they going to do about him?

I don't know. If I'd escaped a few days ago when the warrant was issued on me, I'd have been able to get word to them then, and we'd have had more time.

Verity sighed. She wasn't aware she'd fallen asleep until Anthony shouted, *Wake up!* inside her head.

What did you let me fall asleep for? She started upright. *What time is it?*

She waited for the centrifuge to slow, and then manoeuvred through the hatch and made her way up to the bridge. A red light on the communications console was illuminated.

She pushed herself down into the chair and pressed the

play button.

A man appeared on the holovision screen. "Sergeant Verity, this is Spokesman Sidney Worrall, from Torrmede on behalf of the Meritocracy."

"Not him," Verity muttered. "He's a wanker."

"MANTIcore has brought the matter you reported to our attention. A veto was recently carried among the Spokesmen for the Meritocracy. We have decided that your report demonstrates cause for concern. We are sending immediate orders to Callisto that Farron be suspended from his duties and held in custody, and we have dispatched a sortie from Earth to Callisto to further investigate the matter. The sortie should arrive within twenty days, and has been instructed to secure the base."

Oh, no, no! That's not good enough! They won't be here in time!

No, they wouldn't. Verity realised what he meant. Twenty days was too late by far. Referendum day would have been and gone. Autonomy would have been voted in, by what would seem to the Meritocracy from the outside to be the valid but rather misinformed choice of the local electorate would become law, confusing the matter and delaying things, buying Farron more time.

"Upon the securing of the base, it is requested that you rendezvous with the sortie on the surface as a necessary witness."

It's not good enough, Verity thought. *What are we going to do?*

There's nothing anyone can do. The technology doesn't exist to build fusion engines powerful enough to get from Earth to Jupiter in less than twenty days. We're screwed.

"As for the request you made, regarding the whereabouts of Vladimir... however that's pronounced... there is a PhD student of that name in the research group of geneticist

Professor Eglin. Eglin's confirmed his current location as on Callisto. Sidney Worrall, over."

So Vladimir hasn't been recalled to Torrmede?

The red light came on the console again. Verity frowned at it. *There's another message.*

Open it.

She pressed the button, and up came the holovision image of another man. From his physiognomy, Verity guessed that at least some of his ancestors must have been Japanese.

"This is Takahashi Tōru from Torrmede. The content of this message is private and is intended for Sergeant Zeta Verity of Callisto. Sergeant Verity, from your last message it can be assumed that Anthony Cornelian is dead, and that you have obtained the information incriminating Lloyd Farron that was the purpose of his mission. I understand that a veto has been carried among the Spokesmen, and a sortie is being dispatched to Callisto as I send this message. If the Magnolia Order's intelligence serves us correctly, the sortie will arrive too late, and while the Meritocracy loses time deciding what to do about the problem, we will be losing valuable time which Farron may be using to bolster his as yet unknown forces out here."

Takahashi interlocked his fingers on the desk before him and paused before continuing. "Sergeant Verity, how much importance do you place on the values and integrity of the Meritocracy? Would you be prepared to die for the Meritocracy? Would you be prepared to die *at its hands*, in order to safeguard what it stands for?

"The Spokesmen offer a level of protection to the Meritocracy. They are chosen by the Electorate so that urgent matters that cannot pass before the Electorate by referendum can be acted upon immediately. We are another level of protection, but the Magnolia Order is a vigilante force not under any direct control from the Meritocracy, and thus our workings must remain secret. If you choose to act under the Magnolia Order's instructions, you must bear responsibility for your own actions, and you must not reveal anything of the workings of the Magnolia Order to any person, so long as you shall live."

"The Magnolia Order has decided that this coup must be stopped before it can come to completion. If it is not, countless lives will be lost and the Meritocracy will come to harm. The only person who is in place to do this now is you, Sergeant Verity. Find Farron and kill him." Takahashi opened his hands and slashed them over the surface of his desk, palms down. "Destroy whatever research he's doing. Let nothing and no-one stand in your way. If you do this and you succeed — and your chances of succeeding are no doubt small — but you are not able to prove your motives in doing it, the Meritocracy may decide you are a criminal, and may even put you to death, but if they do that, then it will be your duty to the Magnolia Order to die silent, just as Anthony Cornelian did, and as every member of the Magnolia Order who has died protecting the Meritocracy did. If you attempt to expose the Order to save your own life, you have only my name, and they shall have nothing from me as I follow in your steps to execution.

"I can tell you no more. You alone probably know more than I do about your mission, but to help you I am transmitting all the information we have on Farron and our suspicions about his activities. Over."

The message ended, and the image of Takahashi Tōru disappeared.

Verity stared at the monitor.

It's a suicide mission, Anthony said. *We can't succeed, and if we do succeed, we'll probably be executed anyway.*

"Then I accept it."

It won't make any difference. You'll be killed.

There's a chance, isn't there? And you forget. I made an oath. I swore to you that I would avenge your death. Farron is responsible for your death. I've just been given orders to assassinate him. It's straightforward.

No, it's not straightforward! This is the Magnolia Order you're talking about! Taking orders from them is not the same as taking orders from your superiors in the Sky Forces. If you take orders from the Magnolia Order and then someone questions them, you've no recourse!

Verity leaned over the console and pressed the switch to record a message. "This is Sergeant Verity of Callisto. This message is private and intended for Takahashi Tōru of Torrmede. I accept your orders. I shall not attempt to make contact with you again."

She pressed the transmit button. A light flashed twice. *Look, Anthony, this is your mission as well as mine. I'm going to do it with your help or without it. Now, how do I move this yacht so I can get to the Jupiter orbital?*

For a moment, Anthony did not respond. Then he said, *The course computer can handle it automatically. The orbit data are public information under the Freedom of Information Act. All you have to do is turn the yacht round so the other side of the sail is facing the sun. It's got a CO_2 ballast system. You'll find the wheels that operate the valves on that panel in front of you.*

Verity found the four wheels on the panel, and turned the one to open the starboard ballast valve. A noise of depressurisation, and a jet of white gas appeared in the starboard window. The stars began to drift as the yacht turned.

chapter nine

IS IT THERE?

Anthony's thought: *The course schematic says it is.*

Verity squinted at the stars beyond the bridge window, scrutinising them for hints of which one might be the Jupiter orbital complex. *I can't see it.*

If we could see it, it would be able to see us. Try it on the scope.

Her hand slid to a panel on the left side of the console. When she looked, she saw it was indeed the screen and controls for the magnification viewer. An image came to her mind, of Anthony Cornelian sitting at these controls, his fingers touching these switches and dials and imaging screens that hers now pressed and turned. Those same fingers that now lay frozen and lifeless at the bottom of a crater back on Callisto. For an instant she felt like a trespasser; a murderer and usurper.

The screen came on, and Verity adjusted the coordinates to match the readout the course program gave as being the location of the orbital. Pinprick stars moved across the screen, leaving wavy trails of light in the scope's image. A fuzzy grey torus appeared. Verity rotated the focus knob until it took form as a ring rotating slowly around a central axis. It looked somehow unrealistic and silly, something man-made and dwarfed by distance, laughing in the face of nature's hideous adversity. Hanging there upon the outer edges of Jupiter's magnetosphere, it appeared as a toy tossed from reality and left as a claustrophobic bastion of humanity in between Jupiter's deadly radiation belt and the vacuum of space.

Can they see us?

Not unless they're looking for us hard. We'll have to hope they aren't.

Verity checked the flight schematic, showing the orbiting

path of the complex around Jupiter, and the projected path of the sun-yacht following in its wake. *So, we go there on the lander, and, if we don't die there, we come back and the yacht will still be in orbit where we left it?*

This yacht cost good money! Anthony transmitted in a tone of mock offence. *Stop casting aspersions on it and insinuating it can't hold a stable orbit!*

Back in the main corridor, Verity retrieved the pieces of her armour from the locker and put them back on.

This might be a stupid question, and I'm guessing it's ubiquitous in the Sky Forces, but I have to ask, why are you going commando?

Verity had found a connection cable on board the yacht, which she had connected to Anthony's computer. She secured the Sky Forces standard issue bag with the computer and the other gear in it to her back, and plugged the wire from the computer into the socket in the interface shunt on her forehead. *I forgot to bring any clean underwear, what with burgling Farron's lab and fleeing the base and Sergeant Black's crew ransacking my billet.* She gave her helmet a shove so it drifted into the lander, and took hold of the sides of the airlock door and pushed herself, feet first, after it.

After she sealed the hatch, she pulled herself into the pilot's seat and fastened the belt. It took a few moments for her to start up the flight control computer and get the trajectory plotted. *Here goes*, she thought, and hit the release sequence switch. The belt jabbed into her shoulders as the sun-yacht ejected the lander from its docking slot, and stars and the pastel-stippled flank of Jupiter leapt back into the fore windows. She craned her neck to make a visual clearance check of the yacht through the upper window before pressing the switch that started the course program. The fusion engine fired with a loud roar, jolting the back of her skull against the headrest.

The stiff plates of her armour were unpleasantly clammy

against her skin. Verity fidgeted against the G-force of acceleration pushing her back against her seat. She could feel the angular shape of Anthony's computer inside the bag against her back. *Will you just control yourself and stop being randy? I'm getting bleedback off you and it's not a good feeling when I'm supposed to be assassinating someone!*

How do you know, said Anthony slyly, *that it's not you who's feeling sexy and causing bleedback on me?*

The fusion engine cut off and the acceleration force eased away. Verity reached over her shoulder and caught hold of a narrow strip. She yanked the long piece of material out of the bag: a tie she had taken from Anthony's wardrobe, with a piece of foil taped to the inside. She wrapped the tie round her forehead like a bandana, so the foil covered her interface shunt, and knotted the ends together. Now the ANT on the orbital complex wouldn't detect her, but she could maintain communication with Anthony through the direct connection via the wire.

Don't go broadcasting signals or doing anything stupid in there. She reached back to the other seat and caught her helmet by the strap.

Don't wear that, said Anthony. *You're going to need unimpeded use of your eyes and ears.*

It's easy to die without a helmet. The incident with John Aaron still remained fresh in Verity's mind, and a sick feeling came to her stomach at the recollection of it, despite knowing that John Aaron was dead and had never really posed a threat in the first place.

It's also easy to die if you don't hear your enemy sneaking up behind you! Anthony countered. *Have you forgotten what the Magnolia Order taught you about that katana?*

Verity's fingers closed on the handle of the katana at her hip. *The wise give life with the sword. The fool kills himself on another's sword.*

So don't kill yourself on someone else's sword. Or anyone else's fist or gun for that matter. Make sure they all kill themselves on your sword.

Are you suggesting I don't need armour; that I just go in there wearing nothing, apart from a sword?

Well, I suppose that's a novel strategy. It might give you the element of surprise I guess.

Verity found a smile forming on her lips despite herself, and leaned closer to the window. Details were starting to become visible on the bright star ahead, and it began to look more like the image she had seen in the scope.

It's not very big, she thought as the prow of the lander passed the outer edge of the steadily turning ring, and its perimeter disappeared behind the edge of the window. The radius couldn't be more than a mile. *I expected it would be bigger than that.* Braking thrust cut in sharply, throwing her forward against her shoulder straps.

You're right. Anthony's transmission had a dubious tone to it.

There's no way Farron can have any kind of decent-sized army in that.

We're here now. We may as well see what we can find out about it. I take it you've been trained how to carry out a manual docking procedure?

Verity rolled her eyes and set her hands to the levers that operated the lander's ballast valves as the static central hub of the orbital's wheel drifted slowly in. Hexagonal nodules studded its convex surface — all airlocks for docking. One lander was already in position. Verity recognised it as being the one that had left from Callisto: Farron's transport up here.

She opened the side-valves as the lander closed the distance, to rotate it so the upper section with the hatch faced the docking apertures. After using the keel valve to push the craft in, she hit the switch for the electromagnet. The cabin lurched and the sound of metal striking metal clanged through the hull. The grinding sound of the airlock flanges locking in place began, and the green light on the hatch over her head lit up.

Here goes nothing. Verity unbuckled and pushed up from the seat. She unscrewed the hatch, braced her knees against the shoulders of the chair, then, fingers tensed on the hilt of her wakizashi, threw open the door and kicked up into the unknown.

A short cylindrical tunnel with dimly reflective sides lay without. Verity released her weapon and put both hands flat against the surface, absorbing her momentum before she overshot the aperture at the end.

Cautiously, she inched to the end of the tube, her knees and feet catching the metal surface and sending dull noises echoing through the walls. She brought the top of her head out of the tunnel carefully, until her eyes were level with the rim. She looked out from a concave roof, a honeycomb pattern marking the exits from the docking apertures on the other side. Directly above her position, the central barrel of the centrifuge slowly turned, filling the air with a faint hum just within the threshold of hearing.

Peering around, she saw no evidence of surveillance or other people, so she reached out to one of the handle rails and silently pivoted over on it, so her head pointed back towards the exit. The inner door lay back, flat on its hinges. Verity hoisted it up, closing it over the aperture, and noted the number bolted to its outside surface, 12. She turned the handle in the centre to lock the door, and gripped the rail with her knees as she reached behind her back into the pocket of the bag, and withdrew the piece of paper she'd written inside the yacht. She held it up to the door and pressed her thumbs firmly on the corners to fix it in place.

THIS AIRLOCK HAS AN OUTER DOOR FAULT AND HAS

BEEN REPORTED

PLEASE DO NOT ATTEMPT TO USE

A single pole with ladder rungs stretched from the middle point of the concave honeycomb of airlocks to an indentation in the centre of the centrifuge's rotating wall, about ten feet in diameter. Verity used the rungs on the edges of the airlock doors to swing herself hand over hand over to the ladder, and scrambled down it. As she drew closer to the cylindrical hole in the wall, she began to make out details in its sides. Four holes had been moulded through the solid metal, at ninety degrees. Two were narrow, with ladder rungs curving out and riveted to the exits, but the other two had wide openings that flared backward against the direction of rotation, funnelling into reflective depths that stretched away into an invisible darkness.

It's a chute, Verity thought, pressing her insteps into the pole to take the strain off her arms. *It must run all the way down one of the spokes to the habitable rim.* Above her head, the pole of the ladder disappeared into a hole in the rotating hub.

How are we going to check what's down there? That it's safe?

I've brought a fibre-optic periscope, Verity considered. *But it's probably not long enough, and I won't be able to run it down with it rotating like that.* Her eyes darted from side to side as she tried to follow the motion of the apertures as they turned past her. There wasn't really any option: she would have to go and hope no-one was at the bottom to notice her arrival.

Don't go shouting 'Whee!' as you go, or they'll all hear and we'll get captured, said Anthony sardonically.

Stop treating me like I'm a kid!

You are a kid.

I'm a sergeant in the Sky Forces!

The Sky Forces are just a whole load of kids playing with their space toys.

Verity trod the edges of her heels on a rung and pivoted

herself back by leaning away from the rung in her hands. She fixed on one of the chute entrances as it rotated slowly past, timing it so that she released and leaned in, pushing off as the chute came round to meet her. The rotation ran the sloped wall into her chest, and immediately she began to slide headfirst down the pipe. She put one hand down to the hilt of her katana, her other arm bent up to guard her face, as she slid faster into the unknown.

For what seemed a long time she fell in darkness. The angle of the wall decreased, and before she realised what was happening, light appeared ahead and she shot horizontally into an annexe. The first thing she saw, before her eyes had even adjusted to the light, was a padded wall and a pile of cushions hurtling towards her. She yelled out, managing to twist to her side before she crashed into them.

Verity rolled onto her knees, reaching for her katana, but the annexe was empty. A windowed double door led to a lobby with a metal staircase. She got to her feet and looked through. Nobody there. The stairs brought her down to another double door, leading to a corridor stretching away in both directions. The curvature of the ceiling was ever so slightly apparent, more obvious in the distances where perspective drew the walls together.

She stepped over to one of the other doors leading off, and chanced a look through the window. Science lab: glass and metal apparatus on the benches, far wall lined with fume cupboards, sinks and electrical appliances everywhere. The other doors nearby were also laboratories, and each door had a number. Farther along the corridor she came across doors labelled 'freezer' and 'centrifuge room' and 'autoclave'.

Anthony, do you know anything about what sort of science goes on in these labs?

Could be biochemistry of some sort. Can't rule out genetic engineering. Looks like they're understaffed, unless they're all on lunch or at a meeting.

The sound of footfall and voices became audible, from somewhere in the corridor ahead. *Why'd you have to comment on that? That was just tempting Sod's Law, and now we've got company!*

She scoped a nearby window, not entirely sure the room behind was empty and not having the time to risk making sure. She threw it open and dived behind some lab coats hanging on hooks beside the door, and waited as the footsteps and conversation grew louder, in a stink of chemicals and sweaty armpits. The sounds reached a crescendo and began to recede again, and Verity relaxed from her stiff, flattened posture against the wall.

What exactly are you planning on doing? Anthony asked.

I'm going to find Farron and kill him, like I was told.

You were also told to destroy his research. You think these labs contain his research?

I don't know. The Magnolia Order's intelligence says he's breeding some kind of army. If the rest of the orbital complex looks like this, then taking into account the space needed for the ordinary atmosphere machinery and stuff that's needed just to live in a place like this, there's not room for an army on it.

Then his research might be somewhere else. In which case we'd be best off not killing him straight away, because if we do that we're not getting off here alive, but sticking to espionage until we know more about what's going on.

We have to find the Commodore.

What?

Commodore Smith. He's disappeared. He must have discovered something and suspected Farron, and Farron must have had him transferred up here as a prisoner. If we can rescue him and explain what's happening, he must know what to do. After all, he is a commodore.

The lab coats concealing Verity were suddenly ripped apart

like curtains. She pressed back hard against the wall, hand flying to her wakizashi. Before her, Vladimir let out a loud yell and shot his hand to his heart, a heap of research papers falling from under his arm to the floor.

"It's you!" Verity realised. "What are you doing here?"

"What am *I* doing here? Why are you dressed up like you're pretending to be a commando?"

His comment reminded her of Anthony's earlier one about commandos, and she blurted out, "How do you know I don't have any underwear on under my space armour?"

Vladimir's eyes went wide and his face reddened. "That's really immature," he said, turning away and putting his hand to his chin in embarrassment.

"Oh," said Verity, realising he meant the tie wrapped around her head. "You mean the bandana? It's an electromagnetic blindfold, so the ANT can't tell I'm here. Well, what are you doing here anyway? Have you seen Farron?"

"Farron? The inquisitor? Not seen him since yesterday sometime, on Callisto."

Verity let out a strident exhalation. "He was on the lander that brought you here. You can't possibly have missed him."

"He wasn't. The inquisitor wasn't on the lander. Just me and two women."

"He was going up to this orbital, in that lander that's now docked on the outside. It's part of his regular schedule. He must have been in it, and you mustn't have noticed."

"Yes, Farron, the inquisitor, I know what he looks like," said Vladimir testily. "He's got ginger hair, medium height, sort of stocky. He's got shunts stuck all over his forehead." He brought both hands up to his face. "I'd have noticed if he was there."

"There must have been another room, or something, where you didn't see him."

"No."

"Well, where is he, then?"

Vladimir shrugged and turned his palms upwards. "It would make logical sense, if he wasn't on the lander, and there have been no other landers, that he is still on Callisto."

"He can't be. The ANT there would have noticed."

"This ANT hasn't noticed you're here."

That made sense. But why had Farron said he was going, when he wasn't? And what could he be doing on Callisto? It didn't make sense that he would hide for half of each local day, wearing an electromagnetic blindfold. "All right. Have you seen Commodore Smith up here?"

Vladimir shook his head vigorously.

"So why is it you're here and no-one else who's missing?"

"I got a message claiming to be from my boss in Torrmede, saying I was being recalled because of a problem with my results. When I got on the shuttle, it brought me here, and I was expecting to be put on the next runnership back. But it turned out the message was a fake and it had come from some people on this orbital."

There was a cocky, jubilant effusion to his mannerisms and parlance. Verity said, "Oh yes?"

"Perhaps I shouldn't be telling you this. It's exempt from the Freedom of Information Act on grounds of being unpublished research, so don't tell anyone else. They're headhunters... I mean *career* headhunters. They'd read one of my papers and liked my ideas, and they want to offer me a research position here, conditional on my completing my PhD!"

Verity grimaced. "Doing what?"

"Well, don't tell anyone this either, but they're looking to identify the genes in chimpanzees that are responsible for their strength and aggression, so they can remove them from the genome, and make chimps that are easier and safer for people to work with."

"Right. And you want to do that?"

"Well, I'm not so sure. To be honest, chimps are vicious, dangerous animals that belong in the wilds of Earth, not with humans. But, on the other hand, it might be a really great opportunity for me to get some experience that'll look good on my CV."

"Your experience is in working with horse genetics, isn't it? Why do they want you, specifically, to work on primate genetics? Surely there are plenty of other genetic engineers who have backgrounds in that particular area?"

"I'm not sure. They must have really liked my paper. Doctor Smedley talked about my results a lot. He was an interesting person to talk to. I think I'd enjoy working with him, and it was nice of him to look me up and take such an interest in my work."

"But don't you thing it sounds weird?" said Verity. "Why all the cloak-and-dagger stuff? Why the faked communication?"

"I don't know. I admit, that message really scared me. I thought someone must have accused me of fudging my results or something, and I was going to get hauled up before the board."

"So you left, without telling anyone?"

"Would you tell anyone, if you had reason to think you might be about to lose your job and everything you'd spent your life working for, in an utterly ignominious way?"

"But you left, without telling anyone. Like that's what they wanted you to do. Vladimir, what if they're doing something other than what they've told you, and they're trying to use you to do something wrong?"

"Well, why would they?" He smiled nervously. "What else could it be?"

"What if they want to identify the genes responsible for strength and aggression in chimpanzees, not so they can remove them from chimpanzees' genomes, but so they can insert them into human genomes?"

"Why would anyone do that? Apart from being illegal, it would just make murderous lunatics. The Solar System already has plenty of those."

"What if it was to make an army? An army born to be ruthless and brutal, a genetically modified army of beastly soldiers?"

Vladimir's frown deepened. "That wouldn't work. You're in the Sky Forces. You must know that a military force needs discipline. If they were that aggressive they'd be ruled by their own instincts and attack each other. There'd be no way of controlling them properly. It'd be bedlam."

"This is Farron we're talking about. If the evidence the Magnolia Order has on him is correct, he can make people think and act how he wants them to. He probably thinks he can control this army."

"I've had a full tour of these facilities. It's not big enough to hide something like that. It's all labs and just the ordinary facilities you'd expect to find on an orbital complex. There's nothing of that sort here. And there's no inquisitors' equipment, so it makes even less sense that Farron would be coming up here."

"Then it must be somewhere else! What's going on here must only be a part of it! Anthony — the Magnolia Order — there's evidence that he's doing something out here, and it's illegal and a risk to the integrity of the Meritocracy! And I have to get to the bottom of it."

He sighed and set his fists on his hips, crumpling his lab coat at the shoulders and thrusting out his chest. "What is the Magnolia Order?"

"I..." Verity locked eyes with him, and then closed her

mouth. "I can't tell you."

"Right, well, that settles it. I don't know how you got in here, but you can just go back out the same way. I've been invited here perfectly legitimately to talk about science, and you come barging in here, wearing an electromagnetic blindfold that shows you're obviously not even meant to be here in the first place, and start making these ridiculous allegations!"

"Farron must have been on the lander! He said he was leaving for this orbital! He spends half of every local day up here as his normal routine. There's nowhere else he could have gone!"

"He's not! You've obviously made a mistake, and if you ask me you really ought to see a specialist about paranoia or some other mental disorder."

"Don't talk to me like that!" Verity took a step towards him.

Vladimir raised his eyebrows and pushed his chest out more. "I'll talk to you how the hell I like! In fact, if you don't leave, now, I'm going to put a report on the ANT saying there's a suspected terrorist come aboard without permission!"

This sudden change in him startled Verity. She'd never seen him assert himself. He was tall and noisy, and his slight Russian accent was... *Stop it, Anthony,* she thought.

I'm not doing anything!

Verity shook her head. "You have to come with me! Farron's dangerous and it's not safe here!"

Vladimir let out a sharp laugh. "Oh, really, this is silly!"

"I'll radio Torrmede and report you to your boss for dereliction of your research!"

Vladimir's expression fell.

"Look, I'll try to explain this better to you and go through the evidence we've got, but there's not time to do it here. You have to believe me, and we have to get off this orbital. Besides, I've got a sun-yacht. And it has stuff like meat and cheese and proper food on board."

He set his mouth grimly. "Perhaps it is better I get back to Callisto and get on with my research sooner rather than later. I should write them a note explaining where I've gone, though." He turned and gathered up his papers and his computer, tucking them under his arm.

"You'd better put them in here." Verity hurriedly opened her bag and held it out to him. "We need to climb up to the docking area. And don't bother wasting time writing them a note."

"What if after I finish my PhD, I decide I want to work here? What if nowhere else will give me a job? They'll think I'm rude if I just disappear!"

"Look, I've already told you they don't want you to work here. At least not doing any work you won't be arrested for!" Verity went back to the door and checked left and right through the window. "Where's the nearest way up to the airlock hub?"

"That way."

"You'd better go there first and wait for me, in that case."

Grumbling to himself and lab coat trailing behind him, Vladimir opened the door and set off down the corridor. Verity waited until he was far in the distance before checking carefully in both directions and following. As it turned out, they saw no-one else.

The exit to the airlock bay lay up more stairs, and it was just a vertical tunnel with a ladder leading up. Verity remembered with a feeling of dread the long fall down as she set hands and feet to rungs.

Light came from flat panels on the back of the wall. Soon, Verity's shoulders, back, and thighs began to ache.

"People who live here don't need a gym," Vladimir

complained from somewhere below her.

"Shut up!" said Verity. "What if someone hears?"

"They won't hear. We've been climbing for ages. They're too far away."

"Sounds will just reflect back and forth all the way down these tubes."

After climbing that seemed interminable, the gravity slowly grew lesser and she made out a circle of light ahead, the fishbone pole-ladder rotating slowly in the centre. She hauled herself up and reached out to get hold of the central pole. It rotated against her hand, then she heaved herself up out of the tube and fell back into weightlessness and pulling herself hand-over-hand.

"We can't use that!" said Vladimir as she made her way to airlock twelve. "It says it's out of order."

"I put that there." Verity unlocked the door and pulled it back for him. "Now get inside. There's a lander at the other end."

She waited for him to haul himself gracelessly over. She put her hand on his back as he was trying to manoeuvre into the tube, and gave him a hard shove inside, before pulling herself in after.

chapter ten

"*LOOK AT ALL OF THIS!* Figs, grapes, Martian Red, Lunar Blue, stilton!" Vladimir hung from the fridge with his back to Verity in the sun-yacht's kitchen. "Where d'you get all these?"

"I don't know. It's Anthony Cornelian's sun-yacht."

He held up a dark bottle with an ostentatiously embellished label. "Can I drink this wine?"

Verity shrugged. "I suppose so. It'll take all of the next 24 hours and more to circumnavigate Jupiter and get back to Callisto orbit, and it's not like Anthony's going to want it back. Drink it in the centrifuge."

He floated past her into the doorway of the centrifuge, the wine bottle and a box of cheese and fruit under his arm. Verity pushed her way in after him and started the motor. Vladimir slid up against the wall as the centrifugal force grew, and sat on the bed. He poured wine into a transparent plastic glass and began stuffing his face with cheese and biscuits.

From the back of Verity's mind came the imagined sound of Anthony chuckling. *Don't you think he looks like an ancient Greek? I'd love to draw him in a toga and a laurel wreath.*

Verity stared at him in disgust. "You're still wearing your lab coat! You're not supposed to eat wearing a lab coat!"

"It's a clean lab coat. It's never been in contact with chemicals or biohazardous material! Ahh, it's been so long since I ate cheese!" He smacked his lips, and took a sip of wine, swilling it about his mouth to wash down what he'd just eaten. "So you're saying this inquisitor is up to something, because the *Magnolia Order*," he rolled his eyes, "which I'm not supposed to ask about, told you that?"

"Not just the Magnolia Order. That spy I found." Verity ripped off her bandana and dumped her Sky Forces regimental bag on the bed, pulling it open to reveal two computers with Vladimir's research papers sandwiched between them. She identified which one was Anthony and removed it, disconnecting the jack from her neural shunt and putting the computer down on the bed. "You remember that computer I found on his body? It had a personality imprint on it, and it's been talking to me."

"Personality imprints are just filing and security systems specific to their owners. They don't talk to people, asides from those owners."

"This one does."

Vladimir chewed and stared at the computer. "Why? It's supposed to protect his personal details and his files, not help the person who killed him."

"Perhaps it's because the mission he was sent on here is important. Significant things and objectives that go beyond death could get transferred to an imprint, couldn't they? And it's like Ta- it's like the Magnolia Order told me: I'm the only person who's available on location who has the skills needed for the mission. He needs to help me, or the mission won't be completed, and there'll be a coup, and the Meritocracy will lose Callisto." Verity sat on the bed, next to the computer. "You interface to it, if you don't believe me."

Vladimir scowled. "No, thanks. Interfering with a dead man's computer? That doesn't sound respectful. And when the computer's... *haunted*... well, that sounds downright sacrilegious."

She picked up some cheese and chewed it slowly. Neither spoke for a moment, and the noise of jaws grinding biscuits and centrifuge motors grew prominent in the silence.

Vladimir said, "So if Farron's masterminding this alleged conspiracy, where is he?"

"Are you sure you didn't see Farron on the lander or on the orbital?"

"For the umpteenth time, yes! I've already told you I am!"

He's right. If Farron's not on the orbital complex, he must be on Callisto still, thought Anthony.

"Then there must be another complex on the surface somewhere. But there can't be. Someone would have noticed. To build that, he'd have to ship stuff in; expensive, big stuff, shiploads of it. Prefab units, recycling systems, and probably a fusion engine and loads of pressure tanks and stuff, and then all the staff to install and maintain it. He'd have to go to Earth or Mars to get them, and he'd have to have them ferried here and brought down. Someone would have seen."

Vladimir gesticulated wildly with his hands. "Unless there was some other base somewhere on Callisto that's been decommissioned, perhaps in one of the terraforming stages. It could be possible it's been forgotten about and he's taken over it and had it refitted. It's not unfeasible that he might have been able to smuggle stuff down if it's just parts for a refit, or stolen them from the main base."

"How could there be?" Verity said. "If there were old facilities it would be public information. It would be on the ANT. It would be on the company's report, and I read it on the runnership when I got transferred to Callisto, and there was no mention of anything of the sort."

"All right. Maybe we're looking too far afield. Perhaps there's somewhere within the base itself he's going?"

"What, somewhere the ANT can't detect people's signals? That base isn't exactly small. It's built to accommodate a few hundred, but that's not so big that people can disappear for days on end in it, let alone hide enough people and stuff to organise a coup."

Vladimir threw a biscuit down on the bed and got to his feet. "You're just dismissing everything I say! You're not even considering my suggestions seriously!"

"That's because your suggestions are all stupid and

impractical, and you're just opening your gob without thinking about them beforehand!"

Vladimir glared at her, and exhaled through his mouth, collapsing his shoulders. "Look," he began in a loud voice, "you know the company that made Callisto habitable?"

"Dennis Terraforming," Verity snapped.

"Yes, you were telling me about it when we were getting those core samples. You said the terraforming company extracted carbon, oxygen, hydrogen, and nitrogen from Callisto's crust and used that to generate the atmosphere and power the fusion engine. Where do you think the ice and rock came from?"

"From the crust of Callisto! You just said it yourself!"

"No!" Vladimir straightened his arms at his sides, drawing himself up to his full height and glowering down at her. "Where exactly?"

"How should I know? I expect they just melted it off the surface."

"No, that would be inefficient. It would take too much energy to heat up that large an area and transport it to the site. They will have used some sort of wide-bore drill, like a mineshaft. There's a massive great hole in the ice where they extracted their raw material for the terraforming, and it'll be right under the refinery plant in that base!"

Verity glared at him. After pausing to consider she said, "I suppose they might have done that."

"No, that's what they did do." Vladimir folded his arms, flared his nostrils, and tilted back his head. "Problem solved."

He's right, Verity.

Shut up, you! She stared at Vladimir, and sighed. "I suppose it's a good thing I've already set the course back to Callisto, then."

Vladimir's eyes widened. "You're so rude and horrible all the time! First of all you insult my nationality, then you rip my shirt because of horses, then you come barging into the orbital and rescue me when I don't need rescuing, and now when I help you work out where Farron's hiding you're completely ungrateful and unacknowledging!"

As Verity stared at him, an urge came upon her and she leapt to her feet and started towards him. She grabbed him with a hand either side of his head, pulling him down to her and kissing him forcefully on the mouth. *Ahh, that's good wine, Anthony murmured.* She wanted Vladimir to irritate her senses the way he did her temper. She wanted to spar with him physically as well as verbally, in a contest that would have no winner or loser.

"I think you're deranged," Vladimir said. And then he kissed her back.

To think she'd dismissed him before in favour of *Lloyd Farron!*

*

For a few seconds after waking, Verity thought she was back in her quarters on Callisto, and it was only when she opened her eyes and saw stars moving past the window that all that had happened since came to mind, and she remembered she was lying in Anthony's bed on his sun-yacht. She gave the thought-prompt for the low-level lights and turned to face Vladimir, lying beside her.

"Hope all that cheese you ate didn't give you weird space dreams."

"Cheese?" He blinked a few times, and then he laughed and rolled his eyes.

They'd drunk all the wine. The bottle was lying on the floor somewhere.

"You're a lot nicer person when you don't put up a front

all the time and try to push people away." Vladimir looked from her to the stars turning outside the centrifuge window, a sheepish look to him. "I haven't been with anyone before. Thanks for being... for not being like that about it."

"It's not like I've been with loads of people either," said Verity. "There's only been Gecko."

"Gecko?"

"He's a lieutenant in the Sky Forces. His real name's Dwayne, but everyone always called him Gecko. I never really figured that out."

"Is it because he's a *cunning linguist*?" Vladimir stuck out his tongue obscenely. Verity laughed. He reminded her of the stallion back on Callisto.

"The Sky Forces sent him to Titan. We said we'd stay in touch before he went, but he just ghosted me." Verity had never heard anything back from the last message she'd sent to Gecko.

"It's a shame when things end like that. Do you think that's why you're like... why you push people away?"

"I dunno." Verity considered. She looked out at the stars moving endlessly past the windows with the centrifuge's motion. Anthony was likely right, in that if you gazed upon them long you'd probably end up feeling sick. Her birth had been an experiment. Her genetic father was long dead before she'd even been conceived. She'd met the woman who had donated the modified ovum that was to become her on a few formal occasions, and she'd been polite, showing an interest in Verity's training, but it had been clear she held far more interest in the scientific research that was her career. She'd never had any parental figures, so to speak, and it felt safer not to let people get too close. "I think I've always been that way."

Growing up with all the other army brats, it wasn't the done thing to show weaknesses for others to take advantage of.

"Vladimir?" She reached up to ruffle his hair, sticking up untidily. "You're not coming back down to Callisto with me."

"Yes I am."

"It's too dangerous." She shook her head.

"What, and it's not too dangerous for you, just because you've got a sharpened piece of metal?"

"I'm the Magnolia Order's representative now. And I owe it to Anthony to finish what I prevented him from finishing in his stead."

"Perhaps I want to help Anthony too. And perhaps if I help the Magnolia Order, they might let me join them, and then I might find out what they actually are."

Verity snorted.

"What?"

"I'm trying to imagine you doing iaido. Or kendo. It's not working."

"Will you let me practice with your Japanese sword?"

"Vladimir, you've got a career. You want to screw it up by going down there, and getting killed, or being arrested for spying? It's different if I do it. It is my career."

"Look, if you go down there, and die, or get caught, and get denounced as a traitor to the Meritocracy, what's going to look worse? That I'm down on the base on Callisto, apparently doing the research I'm supposed to be doing there, or that I'm orbiting the moon, eating cheese in a spacecraft registered in the name of someone who was killed for refusing to stop after an arrest warrant was issued on him for spying?"

"I suppose not," Verity admitted. "Perhaps I shouldn't have rescued you, should I?"

"Perhaps not. But then, if what you're saying is true, and the job they were offering me there was to try to rope me in to something illegal, it won't exactly reflect well on me or be easy to explain when Professor Eglin from Torrmede finds out I was on that orbital and not on Callisto."

Verity turned away from him. She closed her eyes, shutting out the motion of the stars. "We'd better start working out what we're going to do and how to get back down there, in that case."

chapter eleven

VERITY HADN'T HEARD from Anthony for some time, and she wondered if the tablet had switched itself off as she picked it up, but the light was still on.

I'm still here.

Verity cringed. *You saw... urh... you watched what we were doing?*

Thanks for making a dead man feel alive again, came Anthony's reply. *And sorry for being a pervy ghost.*

Well, I guess it's your ship. I suppose the thing that surprises me most is how you managed to keep quiet for so long.

Probably, being able to haunt effectively and maintain the illusion of suspense comes down to the discretion of knowing when to be absent.

Verity pulled herself into the corridor one-handed, clutching Anthony's tablet under her other arm. *Okay, so we think Farron's hiding somewhere under the base. How are we going to get back to the base without being caught?*

Check that store cupboard near where you came in, Anthony suggested.

Verity moved away from the centrifuge entrance and pulled herself up the handholds on the walls of the sun-yacht's lobby. Inside the cupboard, towards the back behind the armour attached to the rail, she found a bulky canvas bag as long as a man is tall, with a zip running down its full length.

What is it?

It's a hang-glider.

Verity slid the zip down a few inches. A fine patchwork of silver hexagons of fabric showed inside.

Don't open it in here. You don't want to try folding that

bugger up without gravity. It'll end up jammed in the yacht's main accessway, and there's no spare because I used the other one when I went to Callisto the first time.

Verity eased out the bag and pushed it towards the entrance to the lander.

On the bridge, she checked the sun-yacht's course data on the consoles. Callisto approached, a thin blue crescent on the edge of Jupiter's shadow. The yacht's photosail filled the bridge with golden light. Soon, the ship would fall into Callisto's orbit, and they would need to board the lander and get down to the surface and make it back to the base without being caught.

*

Callisto's thin atmosphere roared over the lander's hull as the broad blue arc grew straighter. Friction brought an unearthly glow to the surface of the windows. Evening had passed and the sun had set in the time they'd been away, and far below, the moon's icy surface lay sunken in the deep shadows of night. Verity steered down, towards the deep ravine at the base of the scarp. Behind her, Vladimir's breath faltered. She hit the switch to start the gyromag motor.

The dark rift of the valley opened before the lander as the altimeter dropped. The craft jolted as the turbulent cushion of charged particles produced by its gyromag thrust caught the rough ice below. Verity concentrated on the green contours the lander's computer had overlaid on the terrain. The trench was nearly completely black, unfathomable in the darkness. Walls of ice rushed past on either side.

You'll need to deploy the braking parachute, Anthony thought to her.

I know, Verity thought back. She offlined the engine before reaching to the handle beside the chair and pulling it up. The chute blew out the back with a thump, the deceleration throwing her forward against the straps. The rush of ice beneath the lander's keel slowed, and the craft slithered frictionlessly over the lumpy surface on its gyromagnetic levitator. Verity took the gyromag off, and the keel ran aground with a scrape and a sharp stop that lurched both of them forward hard before dumping them back into their seats.

Verity unfastened her seatbelt and climbed up to open the hatch. Cold air stabbed into her lungs as she pulled herself up and clambered out. "Give me my helmet," she told Vladimir, straddling the hatch. While she waited for him to find it and hand it up, she once more tied the electromagnetic blindfold she'd fashioned from Anthony's tie round her neural shunt.

Can you still hear me? she checked with Anthony.

Loud and clear.

She put on the helmet that Vladimir's hand presented, glad of the shelter from the burning cold it provided. She switched on the lamp and scanned the rough ice surface at the base of the ravine. "Now pass up that thing in the bag."

After a moment, the bag emerged awkwardly at an angle. Verity pulled it up and dropped it over the side of the lander. "Now gimme your helmet."

Verity jumped off the side of the lander into shadow, and waited for him to climb out. He stood precariously on the top of the lander in the beam of her headlamp, and closed the hatch before sliding down to stand next to her. He fidgeted in his armour. "It's bloody cold!"

"'Course it's cold. The sun won't rise for almost another day." An odd chill that was not from the environment came upon Verity when she spoke those words. When morning broke on Callisto, it would be Referendum Day, and in this, the most isolated of the Meritocracy's provinces, people would be voting for whatever Farron had made them think they wanted.

"Put this on." Verity held out a second tie, struggling to make out his face in the deep shadow of the valley. He frowned as he took it, then draped it round his neck.

"No, I mean put it round your head like I did, so it works as an electromagnetic blindfold. It's so the ANT can't detect us when we're in the base." She helped him arrange it over his neural shunt and tie a reef knot in it.

"Now what?" Vladimir put his helmet on. "How are we going to get to the base?"

Verity held up her hand in the direction of the distant summit. "First, we need to climb to the top of the scarp." She dug through her bag for the bundle of climbing gear, and threw a pair of crampons and a pick in his direction. "Put these on."

"Just so you're aware." Vladimir squatted on the ice with his head bent over so the light of his lamp fell on the crampons. "I don't know how to do this. If you can offer me any hints to guard against my falling and dying horribly, they'll be most appreciated."

Verity finished snapping the crampons to the soles of her boots and tested her weight on them. "It's not that steep, and in this gravity you have to fall a long way before you do yourself serious harm." She slung the long canvas bag over her back, and identified a large, jagged crack running down the wall of the ravine. That would be the easiest way up.

She kicked a foothold firmly at the base, knee bent. Her left hand found a ledge as she pushed up; the point of the pick bit into the ice and gripped. *Pull.* Back leg straight, other knee bent and crampons clawing hard ice. As she climbed higher, crampons and pick rasped on the ice below where Vladimir followed.

She struck the ice with the pick about twenty times before she reached the top of the ravine, where the scarp proper began. An uneven surface a few yards wide lay between the base of the next climbing area and the edge of the crack in the ice, too rough and narrow to ride a horse this way. Verity crouched on hands and knees, and turned to face back down the vertical wall where Vladimir was still climbing. She cracked the point of her pick into the ice by her knees and reached over to pull him up as soon as he climbed within reach.

Vladimir sat on the ice, pick in hand, breathing heavily, ice from his breath forming on his helmet. Verity got up and faced the scarp's base. Sharp, crystalline ice formations gleamed all the way up to the summit, where the bright face of Jupiter peered over.

She put her foot to the base of the scarp. "Come on."

The way I went was easier, said Anthony.

If I parked that lander where you landed it, they might go and look there again and find it. Verity found a spike of ice to use as a handhold. Her neck began to ache from alternating between craning up for handholds and looking down for footholds.

She reached the summit with Vladimir a long way behind. Out of the shadow of the scarp, she switched off her helmet lamp and disentangled herself from the hang-glider bag. She cleared some rubble from a flat area and took a seat, feet resting on an outcrop below, arching her stiff neck.

As often happened in the dead of night, she found her gaze drawn up to Jupiter's full circle, the turbulent motion within the oily bands of its clouds barely perceptible, the famous great red spot glaring back at her like an eye inflamed by conjunctivitis. Twenty times the size of the full moon from Earth, the light it reflected cast Callisto's landscape in a dirty golden twilight, leaving short dim shadows clustering at the bases of ice protrusions.

After a few more minutes, Vladimir hauled himself up beside her. He lay on his back, staring up at the stars as he got his breath back. "Not bad for a view."

Verity reached across and switched off the light on his helmet. She wasn't at all sure that the ANT's surveillance reached this far, but drawing potential attention to their location with lights was asking for it. She unzipped the canvas bag, revealing the shiny fabric it protected.

"I take it we can't just walk up there and sneak back in without being noticed," Vladimir said.

"No. The surveillance isn't great, but it's still good enough that we won't be able to do that."

Vladimir's eyes moved behind his visor. "This is a base belonging to the Sky Forces, supposedly the most formidable military organisation in the Solar System, on a moon that cost who knows how much money to make habitable, and there's no proper security?"

"There're plans to add satellite surveillance and better scanning equipment later. It's not like anyone really expects this place to need proper security now. I mean, the nearest place with proper habitation is Mars, and it only comes into conjunction every two years or so." Verity sighed. "There's nothing here that's really worth anything, not for the sake of coming 350 million miles to get at any rate. Other than the base and the moon itself, and nobody seriously thought anyone was going to try to steal *that*. Not until now, anyway. Since the Dennis Terraforming Company's report didn't show conclusively that Callisto would be able to maintain a solid crust in perpetuity under the current climate management system, the Meritocracy voted against paying for any installations above what was necessary."

Verity slid the long aperture of the telescope she'd brought out of her bag. She dumped her helmet in her lap and held the lens up to her eye, aiming its sight through the palisade of ice spines at the distant shape of the base out on the dark plain. A grouping of irregular blocks formed the main habitation area, with a sequence of domes and connected oblongs making up the research sections. Behind the main complex ranged the exhaust stacks and vast walls of the massive fusion engine that had once worked at full capacity to pollute an atmosphere into existence on Callisto and heat the moon up from its uninhabitable -140 °C, and now continued its function in supplying all the base's power.

Rotating the barrel in the scope's midsection switched it to infra red, colouring the fusion engine with a bright bloom. Scanning back to the habitation area and the main gates, two bright figures stood sentry in the entrance. Guards. Security had been upped since she'd left.

She handed the telescope over to Vladimir without speaking, and turned her attention back to the hang-glider bag. She replaced her helmet and peeled the canvas of the bag back over the silvery object inside, while Vladimir crouched on his knees and squinted through the telescope.

"What is that?" he asked.

"It's a chameleonic skin." Verity had the hang-glider loose from its bag and was trying to ease it open, an awkward manoeuvre given the lack of room on the narrow summit of scarp where she and Vladimir crouched. Before the wings would open, she had to pull out the telescoped central handlebar to full length and extend the main rods that supported the frame down its length. Now she could see the control unit in the centre of the handlebar, with its fibre optic cables running up the triangle bars to the wing fabric. It had interface, but she wouldn't be able to sync to it without removing her electromagnetic blindfold and making herself detectable to the base ANT. She would have to rely on manual instead.

The slight updraught from the scarp's face pushed against the hang-glider's fabric, the bar lifting against her hands. She pressed the button to boot the hang-glider's computer. A pattern flickered on the screen, and the patchwork scales of the wing fabric flushed subtly as the computer calibrated itself. Dark colours spread over the sail's underside, transforming it into an image of the sky overhead.

Will this thing carry two?

Anthony replied, *Air's thin, but gravity's weak. I'm fairly sure it will.*

"What happened?" Vladimir got to his feet, putting the

telescope away. "Does it go transparent?"

"It transmits the light falling on one side out from the other side," Verity explained. "Like holovision. It makes it hard to detect using visual scanning systems, and it's about as close as you can get to radar invisible." She moved closer to him. He was taller than her, with longer arms, so he would have to go behind. "Can you reach around me and hold on to the bar?"

While he stood, much as the well-behaved horses back on the base did, and held the glider in position, Verity secured the straps to both of them and fixed the bottom shield — another sheet of chameleonic fabric to obscure the glider's passengers from below — over the handlebar and shielding her chest and legs. She would have to hope that Vladimir's feet wouldn't poke out from behind it.

When she got into position in front of him and put her hands on the bar, she saw starry sky projected above, and a projection of the edge of the scarp and the dark plain below from the inner surface of the shield. Vladimir's body pressed close against her back, his arms over her shoulders and his hands outside hers on the bar, although she could feel little of the shape of his body and no warmth through two layers of armour.

"You ready?" she said.

"Yes."

"On the count of three, jump. Just let the harness support your legs once we're airborne."

"Okay."

"One, two, three."

The spikes of ice jutting from the edge of the scarp slid out of view, and Verity's legs tangled with Vladimir's inside the harness. The bar vibrated in Verity's hands as the craft hit the updraught from the scarp face.

Anthony, how do I-

Lean into it!

A buffet of air rocked the glider, and the handlebar quivered as she tensed against it, fighting the motion. Behind her, Vladimir's shoulders stiffened, his arms straightening against the length of the bar and nudging the glider back into control.

Verity relaxed her grip as the glider rose. *How the?* "Do you know how to fly this thing?" she shouted back at him.

Vladimir laughed in her ear. "Of course I do!"

"What? How'd you learn that?"

"You were learning Japanese martial arts in your time at Torrmede. Let's just say I was in the hang-gliding club."

Verity had to resist the urge to turn to face him.

There you go. Never judge a book by its cover, Anthony chided.

The hang-glider's nose swung steadily towards the distant base, air currents rippling the fabric that only showed as a faint outlining of seams where the patchwork of chameleonic fabric had been joined together. Wind shrilled over Verity's helmet, and tremors from the motion of the wing ran through the handlebar and into her hands. Lift came like a lessening of gravity in a centrifuge.

"Where do you want this thing put down?" Vladimir said.

It needs to be beneath the watchtower, so surveillance won't notice when we get off it.

Verity repeated Anthony's reply to Vladimir. The hang-glider dipped steadily, the base growing larger ahead as Vladimir's hands guided it on either side of her own.

They approached the base fast now, the white tower of the observation deck standing out dead ahead. The repeating shapes of the prefabricated roof raced below. "Put your feet down!" Vladimir told her.

She tripped over on the impact, and the glider's left wing

grazed the roof with a loud scrape. The nose tipped forward and crashed into the surface, throwing Vladimir on top of her.

"Are you all right?" Vladimir said, as they lay tangled up in the harness.

"I think so." Verity flexed limbs, checking everything still worked properly. "Let's hope no-one heard the noise on the roof."

After unfastening the harnesses, they switched off the hang-glider and folded it back up. They left it under the observation tower.

"That way, I guess." Vladimir turned to the exhaust stacks lurking on the far side of the base.

Verity nodded. "Keep in the shadows and try to stay out of sight of the tower. It's not designed to scan the roof, but better safe than sorry." She picked her way over the roof and climbed down into a recess where two blocks of the base had been joined together, creating a short wall she could crouch in the shadow of. Vladimir followed.

Their course brought them over the research precinct, where they had to clamber between the chimneys of the fume cupboards in the lab block below, and where unpleasant chemical smells pervaded the air. Past this, they crossed the stable block roof, and skirted around the dome that roofed the experimental paddock. When Verity crouched beside the glass and peered through, she saw several horses loose in the corral within. They'd ripped all the grass up and ruined the paddock completely; it would all have to be re-seeded now. And the stallion was in there with them. Putting him with that many mares in that confined a space, and with no-one supervising them, as it would appear, that was stupid. Those horses were going to get hurt if they were left like that. Had Sergeant Black done this? Was she trying to mate them? Was she being lazy and using this as a substitute for proper exercise, without Verity and the Commodore around to question it? A surge of hot anger hit Verity. Those were her horses. She wanted to be there, to see when the first wet, bedraggled foal dropped to the stable floor to rise on shaky knees. She didn't want them to be treated like this, by idiots who didn't understand what they were.

"Let's keep going," she told Vladimir, and continued around the paddock's roof perimeter.

At the end of the next block, the base's habitation area ran out. A stretch of empty ice divided the blocks from the fusion engine. Verity knelt down on the edge of the roof to check the ground below. "Make sure you don't jump down in front of a window," she warned Vladimir. "And make sure you wait until I get out of the way so you don't land on me."

Vladimir rolled his eyes behind his visor. "It's only 0.12-something G out here. It's not going to hurt much if I fall on you from that height."

Verity dropped down, crawled under a window, and bounded over the ice to the base of the fusion engine. She quickly put one of the blast walls between her and the base, and after a few seconds Vladimir appeared beside her.

The fusion chamber was raised from the ice on stout metal pillars, Verity supposed to prevent heat from it from melting the ice crust and sinking it. The pillars had been driven deep into the ice stratum, and a slight bowl-shape to it showed where the heat radiating from the engine had sublimed the ice away in the early stages of terraforming.

Peering into the shadows beneath the fusion block, Verity could make out what looked like machinery, roughly in the centre. As she walked towards it, her eyesight resolved it as a double steel cable running through a pulley system suspended from girders above. The cables descended into a twenty-foot wide circular hole in the ice.

Vladimir switched on his headlamp. The light revealed a furrowed wall to the shaft, the sort a drill might make. When he moved his head to aim the light down the shaft, it slid away into nothing. He moved the light sideways, illuminating a thick pipe running up the side of the shaft and heading up into the engine.

"That must be the pipe for the hydrogen supply for the fusion engine," he said.

"*Liquid* hydrogen?"

Vladimir considered. "Probably supercritical hydrogen. They'd have to pressurise it too much to make it liquid. Those pipes are strong stuff; they're made of single-molecule polymer alloy in sections, but it doesn't make sense to pressurise gas any more than necessary. It looks like they put the storage tanks for it in the holes they made extracting the ice." He stood staring down the shaft for a moment, the light from his helmet vanishing into oblivion. "When you think of all the matter you'd need to create an entire atmosphere... it must be a *labyrinth* down there."

Verity pulled off her helmet. Her breath frosted on her lips. She drew back her head and lunged forward to add force to an expectorant spit, which froze midair, ricocheted off the far wall of the shaft, struck the near wall, and disappeared into the darkness below.

"Oh, that's very impressive." Vladimir folded his arms awkwardly in his armour. "Now if there're guards or someone at the bottom, and that hits one of them on the head, they'll know we're coming."

Verity pulled the climbing ropes out from her bag, and hammered the pegs into the ice at the top of the shaft as she'd done when she'd climbed into the crater in search of Anthony Cornelian's corpse.

"I take it we're not using the lift." Vladimir pointed to the pulley system, and a console on a pole beside the hydrogen pipe."

"No. It might register on the ANT if we use it. You said you don't know how to abseil. Are you ready to learn?"

"I guess I'd better be," said Vladimir, dropping his arms to his sides.

chapter twelve

ABSEILING DOWN WAS FAR EASIER than climbing the scarp. Even Vladimir seemed to adapt to it quickly, and before long they were both at the bottom of the shaft. The lift from the surface, a rickety, cage-like thing with rime all over it, sat in the middle of the space at the bottom.

Verity removed her abseiling harness. Three tunnels radiated outwards from the base of the shaft, equidistant from each other. When Verity removed her helmet, she detected the slight noise of ventilation fans, and a faint draught, emanating from one of them.

"It's this way," she said quietly, putting her helmet back on. Confined places like this, they must need good ventilation if people were working in them. She pondered this idea, wondering if there was any way she could easily suffocate Farron in his lair.

"There's a hydrogen pipe going down here too," Vladimir remarked.

"Quiet," whispered Verity. "There might be people nearby."

The tunnel ended with a blockage of white foamy wall, as though a giant cork had got stuck inside it. The wall had a door in it with a receiver that would open it, if the correct thought-prompt was given.

Anthony's voice spoke from the back of her mind. *You still have that manual override key you graverobbed?*

Verity transmitted an exasperated thought. *It wasn't a grave, it was the bottom of a crater, and I needed it to finish your mission. And yes I do have it.* She detached the key from her belt and sank the plug into the door socket beneath the receiver, giving it a sharp 45-degree twist. The door opened.

Verity stepped through, beckoning Vladimir in behind her when she was sure the corridor behind was empty. The door clicked shut behind him. The walls in this part had been lined with some kind of foam insulation, to keep the warmth in and prevent the ice from melting she supposed. Verity pulled off her helmet, wordlessly put her index finger to her lips, and motioned for Vladimir to follow her.

As they continued into the depths of the catacombs that had lain unnoticed beneath the Callisto base all the time Verity had been stationed here, they passed doors, alternately on either side. The windows in them mostly revealed rooms in darkness, although a few were lit and contained scientific equipment and furniture strewn around, as though the denizens had only recently moved in and had not yet had time to unpack properly. As she passed yet another dark room, Verity noticed an odd glow, and when she stopped by the door she distinguished lights from computer equipment, and many cylinders lit with dim green light from within, like a lava lamp shop.

There was no lock on this door, and it opened when Verity pulled the handle. She stared in the dark room as she entered, trying to make out the shapes inside the forest of glass cylinders. Each one stood on a stub, like the stump of a tree bole, covered with wiring and the glow of indication lights and monitoring equipment. The cylinders seemed to contain water or some other liquid, and more wiring, and objects, hard to see clearly as the room was in total darkness and the bases of the cylinders were lit with that green underglow. As she crept closer to the nearest row of them, she realised what they were; they were foetuses.

The nearest hung supported by a plastic ring secured by spokes to the walls of the tank. A ganglion of wires spread from the mooring, reaching to various points on the surface of the skin. The slimy grey rope of the umbilical cord wound around the suspended body and descended to a pulsating, amorphous mass lying in the bottom of the cylinder. Shunts and jacks and plastic tubing protruding from the living tissue of the placenta led to pipes and cables running up through the base stand. Another umbilical cord — a fibre optic cable — stretched up from the stand and looped through the torus supporting the foetus, up through a ring at the top of the tank, where it curved down and connected with the forehead. The muzzle of the face protruded under the bulbous grey shadows of the unformed eyes.

Vladimir's breathing sounded loud in the quiet hall. "It's not human. Not fully, anyway."

Verity stared at the fibre-optic vine growing from the foetus's forehead, at the point where a neural shunt would go. Involuntarily, she found herself reaching with her fingers to her own forehead, and her neural shunt behind the electromagnetic blindfold. Flickers of colour raced back and forth within the translucent walls of the cable. A chill spread down her back, transforming into a dull ache in her intestines. "It's born knowing what to think."

She started and turned at a muffled noise from behind the door through which they'd entered. Footfall rang dully in the corridor.

Without a word, they both crossed the room to the door on the far side, passing a row of foetuses lined up in order of size. Verity pulled open the door and they darted across the corridor and into another room. She hadn't had time to check through the window first, and they'd entered via a door at the back of a room filled with chairs, like a lecture theatre, and there was a man sitting, back to them, in one of the chairs at the front. Verity froze, dropping her hand on Vladimir's wrist to make him do the same.

The man's wiry sable hair showed over the top of the headrest, hair Verity realised she knew.

"Sir?" she took one step towards him, on the aisle down the side of the room. "Commodore Smith?"

He didn't move, and as she came closer, bringing herself

alongside the front row, she could see how his head slumped against the headrest; the slackness of his wrists on the chair's arms where leather cuffs bound them. More straps restrained his legs and waist, and there was something holding up his head. It was an inquisitor's chair; they were all inquisitor's chairs, lined up like the seats in a cinema.

A goggle-like mask with opaque lenses covered Commodore Smith's eyes, and wires ran up the back of the chair, terminating in foam-covered plugs blocking the man's ears. More wires tangled over the top of the head restraint and connected directly to his neural shunt.

As Verity stared, a muscle in the Commodore's limp face spasmed briefly. "Is he unconscious?" she whispered.

"It looks like he's been drugged," said Vladimir.

She counted chairs. Enough to process sixty at once. And there could be more rooms, just like this. Beneath the base was riddled with tunnels left over from the terraforming. There was no limit. Verity found her eyes wandering from the Commodore's inert figure, following the thick bundle of cables running lengthways along the middle of the floor, to the wall the chairs faced. Lights flickered in its recesses, and screens and keyboards lay about the table before it. Masses of cables scrambled like malignant growths of ivy across the exposed ports, and a faint warmth and hum of machinery emanated from the wall.

"It's an ANT," Verity realised. "He's got another ANT down here, and he's using it for this."

She thrust her helmet into Vladimir's hands, and reached out to the Commodore, meaning to rip those jacks out of his neural shunt.

"No!" said Vladimir. "The ANT will know and you'll set off an alarm!"

She stared at him. "You need to get out of here."

"Verity, I said I'd help you."

"You can't help me. You can't help me go any farther than here."

Vladimir's face grew twisted and tense. "What, you think I'll hold you back, because I'm not Sky Forces?"

"No, it's not that. If we get caught, I don't want him doing this to you. I can't be brainwashed by Farron. You don't understand."

"What don't I understand? No-one's *immune* to indoctrination. You're made of flesh and blood, like everyone else."

"Vladimir, there's something you don't know." His close-shaven pale stubble was imperceptible in this light, and it struck her how differently she regarded him from when they first met, how she'd compared him to Farron and Gecko, how she'd treated him when the horses...

A surge of shame and self disgust filled her chest. She'd ennobled what was worthless, what was nothing, and treated with contempt what was good and worthy; someone who deserved better than that; who was better than that. She had acted without thinking, just as she had when she'd decapitated Anthony Cornelian. And now his eyes, glacial blue, beheld her with a perception she had not before noticed.

"Vladimir, you remember when you came into the stables the first time, the name you called me, Zeta?"

Vladimir's face went red. "I already said I was sorry! The ANT said that was what your name was. It was just a mistake."

"It is my name." Verity sighed. She wished she didn't have to tell him this, but that wouldn't stop it being true. "Well, sort of. It's not a name, it's a number. Zeta comes after Epsilon. Epsilon was the last of Pilgrennon's children. I was born as a genetic engineering project, from the sperm of Delta and an ovum with a genetic code cut and pasted together on a computer. That means I'm Jananin Blake's grandchild. I'm supposed to have genes that make hypnosis and that kind of thing impossible. It was part of the project."

Vladimir stared back at her for what seemed a long time, his face changing from disbelief to pensiveness, and back to disbelief. "Even if there are genes for such things and you have them, there's a massive nature versus nurture argument, especially since this is humans we're talking about."

"Look, I'm sorry, but we don't have time to talk about scientific theories now. I was born to do this; I was trained to do this; and I've got a debt to pay. You don't have any of those things, and I don't want to put you in danger any more. I need you to find some evidence you can take with you to prove what's going on here, and get back to the sun-yacht. Radio Torrmede and make sure the Magnolia Order and the Sky Forces know what's happened. I'll deal with Farron." Verity had a sickening vision of what would happen if he got caught, Vladimir bound to one of those chairs, unable to move while insanity mantras were chanted into his ears and indoctrination images wired directly into his visual cortex, until his own free will was overwritten and yoked to that which would possess him.

"But I don't know how to fly the lander," he protested.

"Most of it's handled by the autopilot. Just make sure you put the gyromag on before you start the engine."

Vladimir bared his teeth in distaste, lines forming on his forehead. "No! I'm not going off without you."

"Just go to the lander and wait. You'll be all right getting out without an override because all the doors have fire escape buttons. If the sun rises and I'm not back, it's too late for me and it's too late for Callisto. The Meritocracy needs to know, and it's your duty to tell them."

Vladimir started to say something, but Verity smothered out the words with her own mouth, wrapping her arms around him, the armour they both wore deadening the feeling of their embrace.

She pulled away from him and stepped back. He didn't take his eyes away from her as she backed towards the door. She jacked the override into the port and turned it, and then she was through and the door divided him from her. As she moved into the corridor, hand on her katana and keeping against the wall, she realised she didn't have her helmet. She'd given it to Vladimir. That meant an unpleasant ride back to the lander, if she did get out of here alive. She considered going back for it, but fear of being unable to leave him again put the idea from her mind.

You know, what you told him was a load of bollocks really? Scepticism tinged Anthony's thought. *Genes won't safeguard you from what Farron does.*

You don't know that; you're not a scientist. I was made as an experiment, and the person who ran the lab's theory might have been right.

Well, yes I do know that, actually. You think only one experiment of that nature was ever attempted? The Magnolia Order have thought of that already.

I was told they wouldn't be pursuing the research any further. What are you saying?

There wasn't just one research group. There were two rival ones fighting over the funding. You think you're oh so special and facing all this angst by yourself, that no-one else in the history of life on Earth has ever had to deal with. But you're not.

Verity stopped, hand touching the cold wall. *So what? Now you're saying* you're *an experiment?*

You just told him you were Delta's progeny. The research group that created you managed to get some kind of highly unethical monopoly on Delta and Epsilon's genetic code. My research group used Gamma's DNA instead. If you're Zeta and there aren't any others I don't know about, of which I am not at all convinced, then I am Iota.

What? How can you be Iota? Iota is the third letter after zeta, and you... Anthony Cornelian was older than I am!

The research group that made you got the funding for the genetic stuff first, immediately after the law against human genetics experimentation was relaxed. After they'd made an embryo, they didn't have funding for the next part, and the law at the time was unclear. So the embryo that later became you went in the freezer. A few years later, the rival company got funding and permission for genetic research and implantation and created myself and two others. A few years after that, the first company got more funding and implant permission.

But that... that means you're my cousin! "I have... I had... a cousin?" Verity's vision blurred. She had to take off her glove to wipe her eyes. She'd always thought she had no living relatives.

You have other relatives too. I'll tell you about them later.

I killed my own cousin?

You didn't kill your own cousin; Farron killed your cousin. Now let's get the hell on with this and kill Farron and finish this mission!

Verity put her glove back on and straightened up, pushing her back in against the wall. Another door stood at the end of the corridor.

Farron's main lab is that way. Anthony directed her. *Down another corridor and on the left.*

She went to the door, opened it with the override key, and stepped through. She paused. Something felt wrong.

Anthony, you've never been here. Not while you were alive, and not as a ghost on a computer. How can you know the right way to go?

I... Anthony thought, but it seemed he couldn't finish. *I can't remember. There's something wrong. Don't listen to me, Verity!*

Don't listen to you? What did that mean? Could a computer be brainwashed? With a cold sensation, she recalled the head on the bench in Farron's lab, the head Farron claimed he had disposed of; Anthony Cornelian's brain and what Farron had been doing to it, which she hadn't been able to bear thinking about. That was why Farron had kept Anthony's brain alive. He wanted to plant lies in it. He'd *intended* for the brain to be recovered, and possibly interrogated by another inquisitor and the lies extracted, perhaps in order to obfuscate the evidence against him. Knowledge of the hidden tunnels below must have got in through bleedback, and then everything had been transferred onto the computer when he had last interfaced to it, just before Verity's hand put an end to his suffering. *Everything, the truth, the lies, the bleedback...*

Behind her, a door crashed open. She spun about to face Lloyd Farron, wearing his heavy fur-collared coat and an insincere smile. Two guards stood in the doorway, either side and just behind him. "Sergeant Verity! How nice of you to come and visit!"

Verity said nothing, but her right hand fell at once to the hilt of her katana.

Farron's phony expression dropped. "Although I must say your manners leave a lot to be desired. *Ad rem.*" He indicated with both hands to the two guards flanking him. "Get her. *Alive.*"

One of the guards stepped forward. Verity's feet fell into position and her katana soared from its sheath. Her blade glanced off the guard's breastplate and tore his throat open. He collapsed to the floor, eyes rolling and mandible hanging in two halves, blood gushing from his neck.

The other man took a step forward, his eyes sliding hesitantly from Verity's face, down, to take in the bloodied length of steel poised in her hand. His gaze moved to Farron, who turned his eyes upwards and twisted his mouth impatiently.

The voice in the back of her mind said, *Verity, you have to disconnect from me, now! I might have been conditioned to say something that will affect your reasoning in this exact situation! Verity!*

The computer was connected to Verity through the wire plugged into her neural shunt. She would have to pull up her electromagnetic blindfold to disconnect it, not that the station's ANT knowing where she was would matter now. Still covering the nervous guard with her katana, she reached up with her free hand and pushed up the edge of the bandana.

A sudden weight forced down on her mind, smothering her thoughts. Searing pain lanced up her right arm, and as her fingers opened against her will and the sword fell, Anthony screamed *No! No!* An intense expression distorted Farron's face, and Verity realised her error too late.

The guard grabbed her, and with Farron's mindlock her training was useless. In seconds the guard had her arms pinioned behind her back and it was all over.

Farron reached up to her head and twitched off Anthony Cornelian's tie. He turned it over in his hands, frowning at the foil that lined it. "Primitive." He bent over and retrieved the dropped sword, and held it up so the light glanced off the grain of the steel and the wet blood at the tip. "But effective. Banks, put Sergeant Verity in the chair."

chapter thirteen

VERITY'S WRISTS AND ANKLES were bound to the chair. A steel belt locked around her waist held her in the seat, and something else that was all uncomfortable metal edges was grasping her around the neck and holding her head back against a three-pronged grip that dug into the sides and crown of her head. Twist and pull as she might, she could move very little from the position the chair held her in.

"You can't do this," she snarled at Farron. "Someone will find out, and they'll make you pay for it!"

Farron was fiddling with something on a table, facing away from her. He threw a glance over his shoulder. "And I'll only do the same to them, and whoever comes after them, and again, and again, and so on, *ad infinitum*. In the end, you're just a *corpus vile*, perfectly expendable. If I kill you, the Magnolia Order will send more. Don't assume our friend Cornelian was the first, and don't expect you'll be the last."

Verity's fingers tightened on the cold armrests of the chair. "The first?"

"They sent two others before Cornelian. The first one I killed, hoping that would be the end of the matter. The second one, well, after talking it through with him, he reached the conclusion that his interests and those of the Magnolia Order no longer coincided." Farron's eyebrows flicked up. "After that enlightening experience, I realised I was going to have to give the Magnolia Order a taste of their own medicine." Farron picked up Verity's wakizashi from the bench at the side of the room, and unsheathed it part-way, examining the grain of the metal.

What did he mean? Was he sending spies back to Mars and Earth, to attack the Meritocracy? Verity couldn't see how that would have any impact, not against the entire Electorate, and not with the Magnolia Order having the level of secrecy it did.

The only individual within the organisation Verity had spoken to was Takahashi, her commander as such, and presumably the only individual Takahashi knew was his superior, and so on and so forth. To infiltrate the Order, Farron would have to send men to kidnap Takahashi, drag him back here, interrogate him to find the identity of his superior, and then repeat the process until he worked his way up the chain to identify the true leader. Verity realised this must be exactly why the Order had structured itself in such a way. When one's opponent is a man who can prise open a mind at will, being empty-minded has its advantages.

It struck her that trying to discover more information and analyse Farron's strategy was a useless endeavour. There was no way she'd be able to get the information back to Takahashi and the Magnolia Order; if the scientists who'd created her had been wrong, she would merely end up as another of Farron's mindslaves. If they'd been right, he'd kill her when he found out the procedure wouldn't work.

"You see, Sergeant Verity, you threw a spanner in the works of my plans." He made a distasteful face. "It seems you go about acting rashly, without thinking first, leaving a chaotic trail in your wake. When the ANT sent out the order to capture a spy, you went out and killed the spy and brought the head back instead. Now, I'd intended to interrogate that spy and, after declaring him not in possession of any stolen information, and having planted some information of my own in him, to release him and let him return to the Magnolia Order, where he would relay certain information to his leaders which, had they acted upon such intelligence, would have been sure to bring about their downfall and ensure a swift and ignominious exposure of the unsavoury nature of this Magnolia Order to the Electorate, thus disposing of a threat to my operations here and creating a convenient diversion. Of course, there was not much spy left to go running back to the Magnolia Order after you'd finished with him."

Verity's temper rose, and she shouted at Farron, "What did you do to Anthony? All that time you kept his brain alive! You did something to him!"

"I decided I could still go through with my original plan. In a slightly modified form, of course. If the next spy the Magnolia Order sent here retrieved not some flimsy information after possibly being captured and interrogated, and contaminated, but some barely-living human remnant of the last spy, from whose mind one of the Meritocracy's other inquisitors had to pry the relevant data, I realised this would give the data in question added authenticity. I kept Cornelian's brain alive with the intention that someone should rescue it. Of course, I didn't expect his rescuer to be someone as close to home as you. I knew you were involved with the Order on a low level; but from their informer I understood it was unlikely the Order would call on someone with your particular... *deficiencies*... for the mission in question. I expected something more precise, another spy getting hold of a cryogenic container in order to transport the head. I didn't expect you to be so rash as to destroy Cornelian's brain and any data in it."

The memory of the dash through the base and the horse chase came flooding back. "If you meant the data to get out, why send Black after me?"

"Because I didn't think you even had the data! Through the monitoring equipment in my lab, I saw you destroy the head! When I saw what you'd done, I thought what I'd done up to that point had been destroyed and I would have to start over with you as the spy-turned-vehicle of misleading untruths. It wasn't until afterwards that I realised you must have somehow persuaded Cornelian to transfer his data onto a computer. Yes, perhaps I did underestimate you somewhat in that aspect." Farron shrugged. "I suppose it helped add to the illusion, at least from your perspective. And the more convinced you are, the more convincing you'll be to the Order."

"You planned this, all along? The whole thing?" The

memory of the conversation with Worrall at Torrmede, the journey to the orbital to find that Farron wasn't there flashed before her. Had he intended all of that to happen? Had he meant all along for her and Vladimir to deduce that the real secrets were down here, beneath the base?

"You think I'd let Cornelian's yacht and his landing craft, the positions of which were there in his mind for me to see, plain as day, stay where they were and provide an escape route, to you or him or anyone else, had it been otherwise?" Farron suddenly lunged forward, leaning over in front of Verity, his hands on the arms of the chair on top of hers, his face inches from hers. The mass of shunts in his forehead gleamed, and his eyes bored into hers with a fierce penetration that was both more intimate than sex and more threatening than a hand around the throat. "You can't hide things like that from me. You might as well try to hide them from yourself."

He stepped away. He took something from the table and put it in his mouth; it was one of the biscuits, the same sort he had in the base. Verity could taste the chocolate from the bleedback, feel the crumbly texture of it dissolving in his saliva. He picked up a mug and drained what remained in it, the mild bitterness of the tea washing away the sugary taste. His back turned towards her, he assembled something from a number of objects standing upon a wheeled metal table.

When he turned back, he had a thin syringe with a needle, half full of liquid, in his hand. He held it up so she could see it clearly. "Sodium amytal. Crude, but effective for the purposes I require."

Although she couldn't turn her eyes far enough to see it, with her head clamped in the chair's apparatus, she felt the chill of an alcohol-soaked swab touching her arm, and the sharp scratch of the needle followed by the burning pressure as he pressed down the plunger and forced the liquid in. Immediately, a dull, fuzzy sensation began to build up in her head. Her limbs started to feel heavy and feeble. "It won't work," she murmured.

"Why not? You think you're special, that you're better than other people? That hypnosis can't possibly happen to you, just because you're you and Fate has decreed it won't happen, same as you won't be part of the statistic that dies in a freak accident, or the statistic that gets caught committing crimes?"

"I'm Blake's direct descendant. I was engineered for it."

"Ah yes, Blake's descendant. It will be interesting to see how much this will take."

"I was made to be incorruptible!"

"There's no such *thing* as incorruptible!"

"Jananin Blake was pure logic. I am her heir. You might as well kill me now, for all you'll get from me."

"Jananin Blake may have been lots of things, most of which we'll never know. She was rational, I'll give you that. And she became that through hard-earned experience, not because of the genetics she was born with. Jananin Blake was not incorruptible. She was flesh and blood like everyone else. You see this god phenomenon with everyone whose name has outlived them. They become more than mortal. People think they're flawless, and uphold them as role models. Everyone reacts uproariously when someone claims that Churchill made racist comments, or Thatcher took bribes, or Blake was corruptible. Behind all the mudslinging there has to be a husk of truth somewhere. Everyone cracks if you know where to put the exact right amount of pressure."

"Not Blake!" Verity burst out. This was her genetic grandmother, the paragon she'd been measured up against every time she'd floundered in her childhood and in her training. She'd always had to be better than just Zeta Verity. She'd always had to be Jananin Blake's blood. Blake the scientist and the master of iaido; Blake the all-seeing, the rational, the incorruptible. Verity had no excuse to be anything less; after all, she was Blake's descendant.

Farron spun back to face her. "If Jananin Blake was incorruptible, why did she never kill Pilgrennon?"

"Why would she kill Pilgrennon?"

"She hated him. Surely you must know that."

"Because if he hadn't done his experiments, Blake would never have been able to destroy the old order and the Meritocracy would never have come about."

"Bullshit! He'd already done his experiments. That was the reason she hated him! Anything beyond that could have happened regardless. She swore to kill him, and she didn't do it. And you want to know why she didn't do it? Because she was human! A sword is made of steel, but it can only cut as far as the hand that wields it is prepared to take it!"

Farron leaned back on his heels and sighed. Verity didn't know what to think. That wasn't what she'd been told. Was he lying; trying something outlandish he knew she wouldn't trust in order to confuse her?

"Anyway, I've given you my explanation. It would only be polite for you to return the favour. Starting with the name of the Magnolia Order official who sent you here."

That was confidential information, information Verity had sworn to do her best to protect. Immediately, she started counting backward from 100, but Farron's probing thoughts were already pressing down on her own, forcing her mind down the exact synaptic paths she did not want him to operate.

"It starts with a T, unless I'm very much mistaken. Taka... Taka..."

Verity forced irrelevant memories to the front of her mind. The image that had disturbed her so much for so long, of the disembowelled robber as life seeped away from his face, the bleedback taste of the stallion licking the mare, the bleedback from the dog who tried to eat fox scat, anything to backfoot him and jolt his concentration out of focus.

Farron roared with laughter, tipping back his head and exposing the dark fillings in his upper molars to Verity's view, from the lower seated position the chair had her gripped in. "You think you're incorruptible, you think you deserve to be called Jananin Blake's heir? You're just like all the rest of them! You think your disgusting memories will shock me? When I've plumbed the depths of the human psyche in forcing information from the minds of psychopaths; murderers; child molesters?" His hands landed on the arms of the chair again, and he thrust his face into hers, his voice lowering to a growl. "You will have to try harder than that!"

In the instant of disconcertion, the name involuntarily surfaced in Verity's awareness.

Farron snapped his fingers. "Takahashi!" he shouted, and withdrew. "*Quod erat demonstrandum.*"

Verity stared at him. How was it possible for him to simply wring it out of her like that? How could he do that? Why couldn't she stop him?

"Oh, poor Verity!" Farron held up his hands in a beseeching sort of posture. "Haemorrhaging information you promised them you'd keep safe! Now what's his first name? He is a him." His eyes widened, his teeth bared and his forehead creasing under the multitude of implants. Verity tried at once to stop herself from thinking of the name, Takahashi — what was it? "Oh, you can't remember. Never mind, I'm sure it will come back to you eventually."

He leaned back down over her, his eyes locking on hers, and Verity fought against the feelings he elicited in her. It was a struggle to get her mouth to form the word, "*Bleedback.*"

"Bleedback?"

She held him back long enough for the thought to take logical form. "From all the psychopaths and murderers and child molesters. It's got into you. It's given you a piece of each of them. Piece by piece, that's driven you insane."

Farron dipped his chin and raised his eyes to her whimsically. "Oh, you don't really think that. I know all you're really thinking about is what happened back in the corridor, before you'd worked out what I was up to."

She said nothing. All of her concentration was occupied in trying to stay in control. Farron moved his face closer to hers.

"*Don't.*"

"Don't what?"

"Don't dare. I'll bite you."

"No you won't."

Verity squeezed her eyes shut as his lips met hers. She tried to be as a stone, unmoved by his touch, but she could not do it. She wanted to clamp down her teeth hard and bite through his tongue when he thrust it into her mouth, but she couldn't move the muscles that would do it. She wanted him dominating her like this, although it made no sense, and he was dangerous and unpredictable, and sexy and utterly engrossing and addictive.

Lloyd pulled away abruptly, leaving every nerve in her singing like a tuning fork.

"Ah well, enough playing around. Time to get down to business. On to level two." He'd gone over to a table, and he was already upending a bottle and filling another syringe.

"Level two?" said Verity, confused.

"That was level one."

A dim hope kindled in Verity. She must have resisted sufficiently to move on to level two. If that was the case, perhaps there was the chance the people who genetically engineered her had been right, and she could keep resisting him.

Farron must have sensed this. "*Nil desperandum.* If you don't yield to level two, there are another three levels of it. And if you won't yield to all five levels of the chair, there is always the *table*."

A cold thrill crawled up Verity's spine and over her scalp; maybe it was bleedback from him; maybe it was just the way he'd said the word. "You think a discussion about dining furniture's going to frighten me?"

Farron chuckled. "There's a lot of guff and bravado about you, Verity." He tapped the side of his head with his middle finger. "Only, I know what's happening up here."

"Then what happens if I won't yield to the table?"

He closed his eyes and exhaled through his nose. There was something smug and arrogant in his demeanour. "There are twelve levels of the table. No-one has ever got past six."

Verity stared at the syringe in his hand as he adjusted the plunger, squeezing out the tiny bubble of air trapped where the needle connected. A thin strand of fluid plumed from the point, dispersing in the air before it could reach the floor.

"I'm not like other people," she said.

"We shall see."

A great thump rattled through the corridor and shook the floor, and Farron leapt back from the chair. Broken glass jangled on the floor and a hot draught and a stench of burnt plastic ripped into the room. Before Verity had worked out what had happened, Farron let off a yell and was out the door behind the chair, in the corridor where men's voices shouted.

He'd run off — some crisis was happening and he'd not even thought to release her from the chair. "Lloyd, you coward!" Verity wriggled and pulled against the restraints, but she couldn't get free, and she couldn't move her head. With her vision limited to the motions her eyes were capable of, she could see the syringe lying on the floor where he'd dropped it. Flames licked behind the hole where the window had been in the far door, and already she could feel the fierce heat radiating from the corridor on the exposed skin of her face. She fought against the chair's grip to no avail. She thought of the flames coming closer, the heat growing worse... she did not want to die this way! She looked frantically to the things on the bench, the swords she couldn't reach, and the bag and the computer with Anthony's ghost on it.

"Anthony!"

Was he aware of any of this? That computer had no other input peripherals, so far as Verity was aware. Did he know of what approached? The computer lay on the bench, inert, its blank screen reflecting the flicker of flames.

A barking, roaring sound made her start. Was the fire getting worse? The flames behind the door faltered, and the noise came again. The flames guttered under a torrent of white air, falling back.

Someone threw open the door, and the shape of a man emerged from the smoke; a tall man in Sky Forces armour, carrying a heavy red cylinder with a black nozzle.

"Vladimir!"

"In Soviet Russia," he shouted over the roar of his fire extinguisher, "hydrogen blows up you!"

chapter fourteen

"WHAT DID YOU DO?"

Vladimir dumped the fire extinguisher and the helmets on the floor as he hurried over. "There was a depressurisation system in one of the labs coming off the main supercritical supply pipe." His fingers fumbled at the straps holding Verity's wrists down. "Looks like they need hydrogen gas for some kind of research. I dismantled the safety valve and left the tap running, so it backfilled the room with hydrogen. It must have made a spark when one of them came looking for me and opened the door."

Verity ripped the collar away from her neck as soon as her hands were free. When she got up, an aching weight deadened her arms and legs, and the room swam a little. She felt like she had after drinking the wine on Anthony's yacht. She synced herself to Anthony's computer before shoving it back into the bag and pulling it up onto her shoulders.

What's happened? What did he do? Anthony demanded.

Verity gathered up her katana and wakizashi. Vladimir caught her elbow as the room began to slide sideways. "Are you all right?"

"He injected me with something."

What? Verity, what did he inject you with?

I don't know. Sodium something. He was going to inject me with something else, but Vladimir caused an explosion and he dropped it. Her sight fell to the syringe on the floor. She held on to Vladimir, her helmet clutched under her free arm as he hauled her and the fire extinguisher through the door Farron had left by.

Are you sure he didn't inject you with anything else?

"No, I don't remember another one."

How far did he get?

"He just made me answer some questions. He said something about moving on to level two."

You're sure?

The corridor was stiflingly hot, obscured by a haze of smoke. "I don't know."

Verity, you have to be sure! If we go back to the Magnolia Order and we tell them not what happened, but what Farron wants us to think happened, we will only make things even worse!

"Verity, please stop talking!" said Vladimir. "You're not making any sense and someone might hear us. Can you remember the way out of here?"

Verity blinked and shook her head. *Concentrate.* These effects she was feeling must be from the drug, or the smoke, or both. "The Commodore," she remembered. "We have to help Commodore Smith!"

"Okay," said Vladimir in a calm voice. "Can you think of the way back to the room where we saw him?"

The corridors seemed different in the smoke, and the fires were still burning, and it dawned on Verity that at any minute the power supply to the underground base might be cut off, leaving them to struggle in darkness. She could sense an ANT signal, but it wasn't the same ANT as the one in the main base and it wouldn't respond to her thought-prompts.

"I'm not sure," she said at length. *Anthony, do you know?*

I can only sense what you sense. I've no idea where I am.

Vladimir cleared his throat. "Okay." His voice was still calm, although his face wasn't. "Let's keep going this way and hope we see something that nudges one of our memories."

As they continued, both of them started to cough. They reached a junction where the corridor joined another.

Verity frowned. This was familiar. "It's this way, I think."

Not much farther they came to one of the laboratory doors. "Through here." Vladimir pushed open the door — which led to the foetus room. The explosion had caved in the far wall, toppling most of the artificial uteri. The foetuses lay amongst the shards of their tanks in puddles of spilt amniotic fluid, most of them not moving, some of the bigger ones wheezing or squeaking faintly with lungs unprepared for the air outside. Flames danced on the wet floor near where the wall had collapsed. The air had a thick acrid stench, and neither of them could speak without coughing.

Vladimir put his foot on one of the smaller dead foetuses, and bent over and tore the arm off it.

"What are you doing? Don't be disgusting!"

"I'm getting evidence to take back! There's DNA in its cells that will prove they've been doing illegal genetic manipulation."

"Oh, sorry."

Vladimir wrapped the bloody morsel in a paper tissue and stuffed it in the front pocket of Verity's bag.

Urh, thought Anthony.

Quite.

They crossed the room and went through the far door, and through the corridor to the room with the chairs in it. Commodore Smith was still strapped to his chair at the front of the room, sedated and apparently oblivious to the smoke. Verity and Vladimir unfastened the straps, but the Commodore's head lolloped to one side when Verity freed it from the restraint and pulled off the goggles.

"Commodore Smith! Wake up!"

Vladimir tapped the Commodore's cheek with the flat of his fingers. The man murmured and his eyelids fluttered slightly.

"Come on," said Verity, and she pulled his arm over her shoulder and turned away, hoisting him up from the chair. "Sir, can you hear me? Sir, we're in danger and you need to stand up. Help me carry him, Vladimir."

As Vladimir tucked himself under the Commodore's other arm and they manoeuvred him about to face the door, the lights in the room went out. "Shit!" said Verity.

"Let's use the lights on out helmets," Vladimir said.

Of course. Why hadn't she thought of that?

Verity put her helmet on and switched on the lamp as they hauled the Commodore back through the corridor and across the smoke-filled foetus room, the dead foetuses and broken glass macabre and gruesome in the light their helmets cast. Smith made hardly any effort to support himself or walk, and the exertion forced Verity to breathe in far more of the filthy air than she would like. Vladimir vented the fire extinguisher at the flames, but it no longer had the pressure it'd had earlier, and the carbon dioxide dribbled from it rather than blasting back the flames. By the time they got out of the room she was coughing uncontrollably.

They reached the end of the complex at last and were out in the base of the lift shaft. The ventilation had concentrated the smoke here, and it was funnelling up the shaft like a chimney. They dragged the Commodore into the lift and Vladimir hit the panel that would send it up to the surface.

The lift rose, its metal panels rattling unsteadily. The air grew cleaner higher up, but still Verity could not stop coughing. Smith seemed to have recovered partially from his sedation, and he choked feebly, eyes streaming. As they got off the lift and onto the ice of the surface, Verity slid him off her shoulder and pulled her helmet off, coughing and pulling in great draughts of freezing air that left her throat raw, feeling as though she'd never be able to oust the choking itch from her lungs.

Vladimir stood with his hands on his knees, coughing and hawking up phlegm that froze as soon as it hit the ice. Verity at last managed to quell the coughing and take an uninterrupted breath in. "We can't leave hi—" she said, pointing to the Commodore where he lay on the ice, but the effort of speaking brought on more coughing.

Vladimir nodded. They pulled Smith back up to his feet and started towards the base. Every so often one of them would have to stop, racked by coughing, but gradually it began to subside. Verity could sense the base's ANT, but it wouldn't respond to her. She must have been removed from the personnel list. Somehow it felt like a personal rejection.

They reached one of the rear entrances, and Verity had to use the override switch on it so they could get in. They deposited Smith on the floor as soon as they had the door shut. He was wheezing and coughing feebly, his arms and legs making sluggish, uncoordinated movements. Verity was afraid he would choke, unable to clear his lungs under the effects of the sedation, but she couldn't think of what to do to help him. Vladimir helped her turn him into the recovery position. They would just have to leave him here, and hope that someone would find him and he would be all right.

Verity straightened up. "We're going to need horses to get back to the lander, so let's go to the stable block. It's not far from here, just up the corridor."

"Right, then. Let's go there. And let's go slowly and cautiously and be quiet about it."

"You don't need to hold my hand any more," said Verity as they set off. "I think the drug has worn off and I'm all right now."

Vladimir loosened his grip and dropped his arm to his side, and it occurred to Verity that she preferred it as it was. "Actually…" she closed her hand around the wrist of his glove.

He glanced at her and smiled awkwardly. "All right, then."

A door flew open and Farron crashed into the corridor in front of them. He breathed fast and stridently, and there was a gun in his hand. "You think I'm going to let you off at level two?" He broke into a brief spate of coughing, and added, "*Ex nihilo nihil fit.*"

Verity let go of Vladimir and immediately shot her hand to the hilt of her katana, but her elbow froze rigid. Farron's stare cut into her.

Kill him! Anthony screamed in the back of her mind.

But she couldn't draw the sword. Her muscles wouldn't respond.

Vladimir shouted, and he staggered forward with the fire extinguisher. He swung it up, slamming the base into Farron's diaphragm. Farron tripped backwards, arms folding around the heavy cylinder as he crashed to the floor, eyes wide and mouth groping soundlessly for words he didn't seem able to speak. Vladimir grabbed Verity's arm and pulled her away, up the corridor that led to the stable block.

A sudden fear came upon Verity that Farron might be mortally injured, and she turned back to look, dragging on Vladimir's arm.

"What you worried about *him* for?" Vladimir said, hurrying on so she stumbled and was forced to look ahead of them once more.

"I... I don't know."

That's what he does, thought Anthony Cornelian's ghost. *Don't think what he wants you to think!*

"Let's just get out of here before he does anything else," Vladimir said.

"No." Verity bent over and coughed hard, so hard her vision went dark for a moment and her stomach heaved. "I've to kill Farron, like I told the Magnolia Order I would."

"Oh don't be ridiculous!" said Vladimir. "What chance do we stand against him in this state?"

He's right, Verity, Anthony thought. *You've got your evidence. You've destroyed his work. If what you say is correct, he's failed to brainwash you. You're uncontaminated and you have everything the Magnolia Order needs to incriminate him. Let's not risk it any more by going looking for him and giving him the chance to take that back from us. It's not like there's anywhere he can hide out here, or anything he can use to defend himself. He's stuck here as a sitting duck until the Meritocracy's big guns turn up.*

They reached the stable door and flung it open. There were no horse sounds to greet them, no background broadcasts of idle socialising. All the stables stood empty, the tack missing from the racks opposite.

"They must have evacuated them," Verity realised. "We're going to have to walk it." Walking would take more than an hour. Without horses, they'd be easy to catch, but there was no other option.

"Okay, out the stable door."

Outside, the light of a dawn not yet broken hung upon Callisto's icy horizon. Verity jammed on her helmet to protect her from the razor-sharp chill in the air. They ran for the main gates in great leaping strides in the low gravity. The scarp seemed so far away as they passed through. It would take too long to run all that way. They didn't stand a chance.

"Halt in the name of the Meritocracy!"

Verity froze. She sensed the tremor of many hoofbeats on the ice through the soles of her boots, and when she turned, the whole cavalry was coming round the side of the perimeter fence to intercept them both. Sergeant Black came at the front, on the alpha mare, and beside and a little behind her rode one of the newcomers whom Verity didn't recognise. Obviously he thought himself very important and knew little about horses, because he was riding on the stallion.

The other riders came about in a coordinated arc to cut them off from the base and surround them. As they closed their ranks and pressed in towards her and Vladimir, Verity unsheathed her katana. If she was to die today, she was going to take some of them with her, and she was going to make damn well sure they had to kill her properly, with guns, because she did not intend to be a decapitated head on Farron's bench.

"Drop your weapons, Sergeant Verity. You're surrounded," said Black.

The man on the stallion raised an electroshock gun, and aimed it at Verity's head.

And the first sun ray of a new day on Callisto glimmered on the horizon, sparkling on the frosted coats of the horses and the icy plain.

chapter fifteen

THE SIGHT OF THE SUNRISE stirred strange emotions in Verity. Would she live to see that same sun come up over Torrmede once more? Or would her eyes be blind, her mind converted to a vessel of poison to be used against her people, to buy Farron time? Would she look upon the sunrise and it mean nothing to the person she had once been; would her eyes be no more than the cameras that informed a robot?

16.7 Earth days. 400 hours. A drop of molten light, brimming on the horizon.

"Put it down, Verity!"

The first rays of a new dawn spilled out over the icy plain, sending long fingers of shadow reaching towards the horses and people gathered before the base. The sunlight had a thin, watery quality, light that had travelled nearly five hundred million miles to reach this cold place. The sunrise lent the landscape an eerie, cheerless quality.

"Verity, put it down!"

Verity moved her eyes from the sun to take in the man looking down at her from the shoulders of the stallion, and the gun in his hand. These horses, whom she'd trusted with her life time and time again; these noble beasts she knew better than anyone, now being used against her by those with no such understanding.

She let the blade of her katana drop until it met the fingers of her left hand. Balancing the sword on upturned palms and without averting her eyes from the face of the man, she lowered it as though to put it down carefully, angling it as she did so the bright grain of the steel caught the sunlight, sending a dazzling reflection racing up the blade and into the face of the stallion standing in front of her.

His eyes wheeled to the whites, his head went up, and

he took a faltering step back, ignoring a barrage of surprised shouts and kicks from his rider. He shied and turned, crashing into one of the other horses as he tried to escape the scary shiny thing, and cantered to the safety of the building. The horse he'd gone into was the alpha mare, and Verity sensed the sharp broadcast of her anger. The hormones of early pregnancy were in her blood, and these were her horses for her to protect, and she would not have him, a mere stallion, bringing disorder here! Her ears went back, and she ran after the retreating stallion, lunging at his rump with her teeth as Sergeant Black yelled and pulled the reins, face rigid in concentration as she assailed the horse with thought-prompts. The stallion broadcast panic and sped to a gallop, unseating his rider. The other horses began to mill about in confusion as they tried to follow their leader.

Verity sprang upright, resheathing her katana, and seized the nearest horse by its bridle. She turned its head to her as its rider fumbled for his gun. She got the faceplate undone, synced herself to the horse, and immediately gave the thought-prompt to rear up. The next moment, the rider was on the ice on his back, and Verity was vaulting into the saddle. "Get a horse!" she shouted to Vladimir.

He had one by the bridle, and Verity gathered up the reins as she moved her own horse alongside, grabbing its rider's arm and moving away so he unbalanced and fell to the ground. "Come on!" As soon as Vladimir had mounted, she led his horse by its bridle as she gave hers the command to move away, trying to get them both clear of the commotion. She released it once he was into its stride and they were clear of the others.

"Keep close to me and make for the scarp!" she called to him as the horse rose to a gallop.

Not bad, for someone the Magnolia Order reckoned wasn't up to this mission, thought Anthony from inside the bag.

You can tell them that yourself when we get back.

"There's someone following us!" Vladimir shouted.

Verity used the horse's vision to look. It was Farron; he was wearing his furry-collared coat and no helmet, and she was certain that was the alpha mare he was riding. "What's he doing?" she yelled back to Vladimir. "He can't control two people and their horses at once, and he'll die of hypothermia dressed like that out here!"

Oh, he has his reasons, Anthony explained. *I don't know what happened back there in his lab, but I'd imagine he rather foolishly went off on a monologue and told you what he was doing before he was interrupted. You now have intelligence he intended to overwrite with something else, and he doesn't want that information to escape. If he can't stop you, it's in his interests to kill you.*

Anthony was right. Verity urged the horse faster, pushing ahead of Vladimir to take the lead on the path around the side of the scarp. The crystal palisades of the ice protrusions rushed past amidst the snorting of the horse and the clouds of vapour it threw over its shoulders with each breath.

"When I jump, jump after me!" she shouted. "I don't care if it looks dangerous; I don't want you to think about it, just do it!"

They rounded the edge of the scarp, and Verity had to duck over the horse's neck to avoid a large ice spike that had come down from the ridge and fallen over the path. They must be nearing the edge of the crater now; there was the place Anthony's body had fallen over the edge. This horse wasn't like the stallion. She wouldn't be afraid, so Verity didn't have to worry about controlling her. She just had to know exactly where the right place to jump was.

"Here! Follow me!"

The crystalline edges of the path caught the sunrise and sparkled as she turned the horse and gave the thought-prompt to jump. The ravine sailed past below. There was the yacht's lander, lying at the bottom a hundred yards or so away. The black ice of the plain below came up to meet them. Verity kicked her feet free of the stirrups as soon as she recovered from the jolt of the landing, and slid off with the horse still moving.

"Don't dismount yet!" said Vladimir. "We've still got a way to go."

"I don't want the horses hurt by the fusion engine when we take off!" Verity argued. "Now get down and come!"

They bounded across the plain, back towards the scarp and the ravine where the lander was hidden. Verity glanced up at the ridge once before she leapt into the ravine, but saw no horse there. *Hurry*, Anthony urged. She landed heavily and stumbled down on her knees, before getting up and running to the lander. She gave the thought-prompt to unlock before she'd even reached it, and then Vladimir was up on the roof turning the wheel that would open the airlock.

She vaulted onto the lander's roof. She was still synced, and in the horse's peripheral vision she could see Farron and the alpha mare up on the ridge, his hair and eyebrows rimed with frost from his breath, fury on his face as he raised his arm and squinted down the barrel of a gun.

"Get in!"

Vladimir slithered through the hatch and into the lander. As Verity dropped her feet through and took up her weight on her arms to lower herself after him, a blow to the back hurled her forward against the rim. She fell into the pod across the headrest of the pilot's seat, with her head in the footwell. Her vision blacked out. He'd shot her in the back, the bastard. A dead mass filled up her chest, and when she tried to draw breath her lungs would not respond. Certain that death was imminent, she could not even muster the voice to speak to Vladimir.

Goodbye, Anthony.

Anthony?

Verity opened her eyes. The lander's interior drifted into focus. She found herself able to inhale, against the pain in her chest. She'd winded herself when she'd fallen on the hatch.

Verity!

Against the ringing in her ears, the voice seemed to come from inside her head.

"Verity!" It wasn't Anthony's voice, it was Vladimir's. He reached over the back of the pilot's seat and pulled her upright by the shoulder straps of her Sky Forces backpack. A stink of scorched electricals burnt the insides of her nostrils. "Verity, are you all right?"

"Uh," she said.

"We need to take off. Now!"

Verity twisted around so her weight fell properly into the seat and pulled the straps over her shoulders. When she glanced up, the green light was already up on the airlock door. Vladimir must have closed it.

Anthony?

She took off her gloves and fumbled numbly for the controls. *Anthony, I can't remember the takeoff sequence.*

"Verity, we need to go!"

Gyromag first, she recalled. Her hand found the control for it. The little craft gave a lurch as the gyromag levitator came online. Now the fusion engine. This felt awkward, like something she'd never had any experience with. The force of the acceleration threw her back against the seat, and she gripped the steering bar, holding the lander's course straight as it chased up from the ravine and the horizon grew curved and blue before her eyes, although her arms trembled and a deep feeling of shock paralysed her inside. *Anthony, I can't do this without you!*

The readouts and course schematics on the screens in front of her finally started to register, and the memory of how to operate the craft started to return to her and form sense. The autopilot would take over in a minute. She just needed to hold the craft still a little longer.

As soon as the autopilot came online, she tried to twist round to reach the bag, but the acceleration force and her seatbelt made it impossible. *Anthony!* "There's something wrong!"

"We're nearly there! See, there's the yacht!"

Verity looked where he pointed, to a bright star in the fore window. Nearly there. Nearly.

Vladimir had his seatbelt off and was standing up in his seat before the craft had even finished docking. Immediately when the light came on the airlock door, he turned the wheel and threw it open. "Come on!" he said, manoeuvring up and putting down a hand to pull Verity out into the yacht's central bay.

She held on to the rail as she wriggled the bag off her shoulders. When she reached inside and pulled out the computer, a dark indentation had burned a ragged shape in the plastic close to one corner, falling in to a hole that revealed warped metal surfaces within.

"We need to get into the centrifuge, and find a screwdriver!"

"What are you talking about? We've got to radio Torrmede and tell them what's happened! And you need to gimme that sample so I can put it in the freezer."

Verity wasn't listening to him. She pulled herself through the doorway to the centrifuge. She found a box of tools in one of the rooms inside, and she sandwiched the computer between her knee and elbow and the table as she took out the screws holding the casing together. Inside, where Farron's shot had hit it, was a deformed rectangular object with its interior metal surfaces all melted. "We have to fix this!"

"That's the hard drive," said Vladimir quietly, from behind

her. "It can't be fixed."

Verity stared at the broken computer, and it blurred before her eyes. "Anthony's dead," she said, and it came out in a sob.

"What's the matter? I thought you already killed him."

"We were going to do stuff together. I was going to make it up to him for killing him."

Vladimir put his arms around her, rather awkwardly without gravity to support them both. Verity put her head against his chest as her shoulders shook and her breathing broke into shuddering gulps.

"Look," he said gently. "I'll go and radio Torrmede for you, if you like. Would that be better?"

"Yes."

"All right, then. What do you want me to tell them?"

Verity swallowed and took a deep breath. "Tell the Magnolia Order we've got a sample and we've destroyed the illegal research, but we've failed to kill Lloyd Farron. And tell them we're turning the yacht round, and we're going back to Torrmede."

chapter sixteen

THE BLADE OF THE SHOVEL bit into the hard-packed earth, and Verity had to step on the back edge and use her weight to cut the ground. The sun was warm, and after a few shovelfuls of earth she was already sweating. She grit her teeth and persevered with the digging, until she'd made a hole a foot or so deep.

She'd given Anthony's computer over to forensics, after debriefing her superiors in the Sky Forces and the meeting with Takahashi in which she'd gone over in detail several times everything she could remember that she'd learnt for herself on Callisto or gleaned from Anthony's ghost. They'd been unable to recover anything from the hard drive, and, as nothing else could be done, it had been returned to her.

Verity straightened up and arched her back. She dragged her sleeve across her forehead, and looked back in the direction of Torrmede House and the sun in the sky, and the bright flowers of the rhododendrons that covered the grounds. A rectangle of lawn separated the house from the magnolia garden, where the trees surrounded the statues at the centre. Normally, the general public wasn't allowed in here, but an exception had been made in this case, by request of the Magnolia Order.

The statues stood on their plinths with their backs to each other, Pilgrennon with a noble expression and his right hand folded on his chest, Blake poised with her hand on the hilt of her katana and a keen intelligence on her face.

"Ready?" Vladimir said.

Verity nodded.

He held out the bag to her, and she slid her hands inside and took out the computer that had been the last resting place of the ghost of Anthony Cornelian, spy for the Magnolia Order. She turned the computer so its undamaged screen faced upwards, and placed it in the hole she had dug.

"Goodbye, Anthony Cornelian." She scattered earth over the dead computer. "No-one will remember your name, but in your profession that counts as success. You did as much for the Meritocracy as anyone ever did, and you deserve to be buried here with its heroes."

"Ashes to ashes, dust to dust, diodes to... whatever," said Vladimir.

Verity finished putting the soil back, and smoothed down the surface with the palms of her hands. Vladimir put a slightly crumpled rhododendron flower down on the grave; white with a violet throat. Then they both rose and looked down on the grave, and Verity turned to look at the statues.

"Farron said Blake hated Pilgrennon," she said. "You think he was lying to get a reaction from me?"

Vladimir shrugged. "He's trained to get information out of people. He probably says whatever he thinks will get it."

"I don't think they hated each other." Verity stared at the statues. They didn't look like people who hated each other, but then they were only statues. "Perhaps they even *loved* each other." Blake had been the first person to have had a Solar funeral. Was that merely because the Meritocracy felt the need to honour her in such a decadent way, or was it what she would have chosen? Would they have preferred their bodies interred in this warm red earth, in the place they loved, beneath the magnolia trees?

Was this the real Jananin Blake, who scored her name into the history books in flames and slashes of Japanese steel; who left the old order trampled and broken in her wake, like the petals of spent magnolias, and forged the way ahead with her words and ideas? Verity watched her still stone face, but she didn't offer any answers. A drop of rain landed on the statue's nose.

"Perhaps we should go and have a drink, or something, for

Anthony."

"Sorry I never got to meet him." Vladimir exhaled and dropped his arms to his sides. His fingers touched Verity's.

"I suppose, he loved life." She glanced at him. "And everything in life that's good. Food. Drink. People. I don't think it suited him, being a machine."

"Let's make a promise to him," said Vladimir. "To make the most and give the best of however much time we get, for him as well as ourselves."

It started to rain harder as they ran hand in hand down to the edge of the rhododendron forest. The smell of earth and leaves and rhododendron flowers was intoxicating.

the end

Also by Manda Benson

PILGRENNON'S CHILDREN

Pilgrennon's Beacon

Dana Provine is an autistic girl with a secret ability to mentally control computers, who runs away from bullies at her school in Coventry after a hospital scan reveals an object lodged in her brain. A compelling signal leads her north to the Outer Hebrides and an abandoned military facility on the remote and supposedly haunted Flannan Isles, where she hopes to untangle the mystery shrouding her birth and her missing parents. But as the lies of the past unfold, Dana unwittingly finds herself the focus of events that will change the future for everyone.

The Emerald Forge

Following the Information Terrorism attack on London, a radical new government has risen to power. The world is changing, but so far as it concerns Dana Provine, an unusual autistic girl growing up in an unforgiving society, everyday life is much the same. When Dana is troubled by disturbing dreams about a hospital, and a boy from school who seems to know far too much about the past starts following her, it's just two more problems on top of many. But when she encounters a bizarre construct, half beast, half machine, she realises something dangerous is going on that could affect everyone. The answer she seeks could confirm both her greatest hope and her deepest fear: that Ivor Pilgrennon still lives.

TANGENTRINE

www.ingramcontent.com/pod-product-compliance
Lightning Source LLC
LaVergne TN
LVHW041704060526
838201LV00043B/571